'Ali—Ali, I'm sorry about all this—that I didn't let you know I was coming back.'

Sam lifted his broad shoulders in an involuntary sigh.

'It was a shock, yes,' she interrupted him curtly. Alison's heart was still racing but she was coping.

'I need to explain.'

'No, you don't, Sam.' She corrected him with growing confidence. 'Remember? We agreed before you left—no more explanations, unless it concerns Gemma. You have your own life now.'

Alison knew she had hurt him. His lean face tightened, the dark eyes flickered momentarily, a paleness shadowing his deep tan. But for as much pain Sam had ever caused her, she knew she couldn't inflict any on him.

Carol Wood lives with her artist husband, her grown-up family and parents on the south coast of England. She has always taken an interest in medical matters, especially general practice and nursing in the community. Her hobbies are walking by the sea, watching wildlife and, of course, reading and writing romantic fiction.

Recent titles by the same author:

THE PATIENT DOCTOR
THE HONOURABLE DOCTOR

BACK IN HER BED

BY
CAROL WOOD

MILLS & BOON®

First published in Great Britain 2001
Large Print edition 2002
Harlequin Mills & Boon Limited,
Eton House, 18-24 Paradise Road,
Richmond, Surrey TW9 1SR

© Carol Wood 2002

ISBN 0 263 17311 9

Set in Times Roman 16½ on 17 pt.
17-0902-50325

Printed and bound in Great Britain
by Antony Rowe Ltd, Chippenham, Wiltshire

CHAPTER ONE

Was it that distinctive reedy river smell, Alison wondered as she sat in her car and wound down the window, or the almost painful scent of summer that opened the floodgate to memory?

Or, more realistically, was it simply the knowledge that after a two-minute walk from here she would come face to face with Sam, no doubt sitting behind his desk, his long body sprawled out behind it in his customary fashion.

Alison swallowed with difficulty. She gazed upward to the ground-floor window, her heart beginning to pound. Reluctantly, yet hungrily, she feasted her eyes on the high stone walls of Lamstone Surgery rising out of the smooth green river.

Her gaze followed the belt of milky white chalk encircling the foundations. Above this, overlooking the river, Sam's room. Capped by a roof of silver slate tiles, the three-storey riverside building caused a deep stirring inside her. Heart, pulse, adrenaline…a cocktail that she had tried hard to resist.

Fighting nostalgia, Alison breathed deeply. This place was and always would be synonymous with Sam. His presence had never left here, despite his ten-month absence. He was, she had been forced to accept, inextricably linked with this small, totally addictive corner of the universe.

'Can't you just see it when it's all finished, Ali? How beautiful it will be?' Sam had once asked her breathlessly, his deep brown eyes full of fiery enthusiasm. The house was so breathtakingly beautiful in itself, her love-drugged mind had never got round to answering him.

A dilapidated nineteenth-century waterfront building had held little allure—only her husband's enthusiasm for it had sparked her interest. She'd been too preoccupied with her pregnancy, totally consumed by the life inside her.

Alison closed her eyes, trying to stop the spinning wheel inside her head. She didn't want to repeatedly go over the past, playing and replaying the memories in her mind. Heavens, she was thirty-three years of age, yet she still felt like a confused adolescent. When would this internal interrogation ever stop? Would she ever be at peace with herself, accept the fact that their separation was the most painfree route to divorce? Best for their daughter, Gemma, best for each other.

A sudden tap on the car window caused Alison to jump guiltily. She flicked open her large blue eyes and gazed into the craggy, smiling face of Peter Johnson, Hector Trenchard's younger partner.

'Seven-thirty on a gorgeous morning and she sits there looking as fresh as the proverbial daisy.' The young doctor arched wry eyebrows. 'What's your secret Ali?'

Alison smiled self-consciously. 'An efficient alarm clock, Peter. In other words, a little daughter who decides she wants a cuddle at six o'clock in the morning.'

'Ah—wouldn't we all?' Peter sighed teasingly. 'Some of us, unfortunately, have to make do with a very unsatisfactory pillow.'

'The joys of bachelorhood,' Alison chuckled. 'But if it's any comfort, I would have given anything for an extra half an hour lie-in.' It was an outright lie, Alison reproved herself. The truth was she hadn't slept a wink last night, agonising over today. And when Gemma had woken at five, she had welcomed her daughter's loving arms around her, grateful for both the daylight and Gemma's incessant chatter.

'Alison?' Peter was frowning at her. 'Is everything all right?'

'Sorry...sorry, Peter,' she apologised hastily, realising she had drifted off. 'I'll be right with you.' Alison pushed the soft curtain of ash blonde hair behind her ear and reached for her case.

Peter opened the car door and she climbed out, attempting to avoid his curious gaze. 'It's the big day, I suppose,' he said hesitantly as they began to walk along the towpath. 'Or rather, well...heck...what am I saying? I mean, this is the first time you've seen Sam since last year...'

'Ten months, Peter,' Alison replied rather sharply, immediately regretting her tone and the first slip of the mask.

'Yes, my first year here has gone pretty quickly for me but, then...' He looked at her hesitantly. 'It's different for you, Ali, of course. I...er...hope we won't be losing you...'

'No,' Alison heard herself answering in the abrupt tone she had tried so hard to conquer when anyone strayed onto the subject of her and Sam's separation. 'Sam's decision to return to the practice won't affect me. Hector still wants me to cover Mondays and Fridays and I'm perfectly happy with that.' Why was she trying to explain herself? There was no need. She had to get a grip to face this without snapping everyone's heads off.

Unexpectedly, the young doctor laid a hand on her shoulder. 'Listen Ali, I'm not prying. I just want you to know—if you need a bolthole, come into my office, go out on the balcony, sit yourself down and ignore me completely. I promise I won't say a word.'

Alison heaved in a breath. 'Thanks, Peter. I might take you up on that. Sorry I snapped.'

'Forget it. Come on, I'll walk you in.'

Alison was truly grateful for Peter's support. She had thought she had prepared for this moment, but she was wrong. Visualising herself ascending the railed walkway and entering the curved, half-glassed entrance, whose discreet frontage Sam had agonised over with the architects for weeks, and never in her wildest dreams had she ever imagined she would see Sam practise here again.

'Good morning, Dr Stewart, Dr Johnson.' Dark-haired Lucy Edwards was opening the glass partitions that separated the office from the waiting area. The young receptionist smiled guilelessly and Alison breathed slightly easier.

'Hi, Lucy. Full surgeries?' Alison heard this stranger asking. It was her own voice but oddly hollow, though thankfully Lucy didn't seem to notice.

'Absolutely. You'll see the list when you go in. But you're nice and early. I'll bring you coffees and get you sorted out.'

'Promises, promises.' Peter chuckled, giving Lucy a wink. 'Make mine two sugars, Lucy, will you? Hot and very strong.'

'You had a good weekend, then?' Lucy's expression was mischievous.

Alison smiled, grateful for the distraction of Peter's mildly flirtatious conversation with the attractive young receptionist, allowing her the opportunity to turn and hurry towards the narrow, half-timbered staircase that led upstairs to her room.

She should, of course, have looked where she was going and not been in such a hurry to reach safety. Instead, she walked into what felt like a solid brick wall that had not been there previously.

Her vision momentarily gone, a flash of light seemed to come from somewhere above and suddenly she was reeling. She knew—but would never admit later—that had it not been for the way Sam held onto her, one arm thrust against the wall to steady them both, the other firmly around her waist, she would have fallen unceremoniously to the floor. Or perhaps onto the smooth padded chairs of the waiting area. Either way, it would have completely shattered her fragile self-image.

'Alison?' Sam's voice, unbearably deep and familiar, floated into her consciousness. She realised she was still in his arms, though upright now, and the sensation of unsteadiness was fading. 'Alison—that was a heck of a bump… Alison…?'

'Are you OK, Dr Stewart?' Lucy asked, hurrying over from the office.

'Yes…I'm all right, Lucy,' Alison muttered, her field of vision clearing slightly as her palms pressed against Sam's strong chest.

'You don't look it.' God, his voice hadn't changed—not even a little. She knew every intonation, every breath. Her stomach lurched at the low, husky tone, as it had never failed to do throughout their relationship.

'I'll er…make that coffee,' Lucy said, and bolted off. Alison looked up dazedly to find both Sam and Peter staring down at her.

'You bumped your head on my shoulder,' Sam said peering into her eyes. 'You gave it quite a knock.' His fingers glided over and landed somewhere above eye level. 'That must be tender…'

'No.' She winced at his touch.

'Fibber.' Peter frowned.

'I couldn't stop you. You were going like a train.' Sam tapped the proud jut of his shoulder bone. Two very tanned, long fingers ruffled the soft ivory linen of his shirt. Involuntarily, her eyes devoured him, every curve, each hard, honed muscle, the proud sweep of chest and flat abdomen that tapered to slim hips and long legs.

'I was just…' she mumbled, trying to disengage herself.

'Just going too fast and not looking where you were going,' Peter said for her in a reproving voice. 'Be warned!' With a light-hearted grin he turned and disappeared.

Her panic increasing, Alison watched him go. There was nothing for it. She was alone with Sam, had to look at him, had to—

'Hello, Ali.' His voice sent shock waves through her again. She turned slowly.

'Hello, Sam.'

His wide mouth curved into a smile. 'It's...it's good to see you.'

She tried to quell the panic inside her. What had she been going to say? She had rehearsed it so many times. An answer that was polite—pleasant even—but held no hint of intimacy. But it had gone, whatever it was. Her mind was blank.

'Can we talk? Not now, of course. After surgery?'

'I...have to collect Gemma.' Her response sounded lame. 'She's with Clare—as I wrote to you...'

'Yes. You said, in your—*three*—letters.'

Heat rushed to Alison's cheeks. She didn't know why. She had nothing to feel guilty about. Sam's regular monthly issues from Australia had probably been a balm to salve his pricking conscience.

The three letters she had written him had all been for specific reasons. Her first had been to explain her decision to return to work. Hector had asked her to help fill the gap that Sam's abrupt departure had left. The second had been to let him know that their daughter had received his Christmas presents. The third had been to say that Gemma was walking. Perhaps the third had been unnecessary, but Gemma had taken those first vital, stumbling steps and her maternal pride had triumphed over her alienation from Sam.

Again they seemed doomed to silence. Sam lifted his broad shoulders in an involuntary sigh. 'Ali   Ali, I'm sorry about all this—that I didn't let you know—'

'It was a shock, yes,' she interrupted him curtly. She had got her breath back now. Her heart was still racing, but she was coping.

'I...I need to explain—'

'No, you don't, Sam,' she corrected him, with growing confidence now. 'Remember? We agreed before you left—no more explanations, unless it concerns Gemma. You have your own life now, you must live it the way you see fit.'

She knew she had hurt him. His lean face tightened, the dark brown eyes flickered momentarily, a paleness shadowing his deep tan. Yes. She had hurt him. As she had intended. Then suddenly what little satisfaction she had gained was gone. That was her downfall. For as much pain that Sam had ever caused her, she couldn't inflict any on him. She swallowed, defeated.

'Ali—we need to talk.'

Her deep blue eyes coolly assessed him. Here stood the man with whom she had conceived Gemma, the man she had loved to distraction and the man who had betrayed her. Once—a long time ago—she would have agreed they needed to talk. But Australia had changed all that. He had decided to place a universe between them, and returning now—whatever his reasons—made no difference. Her space, her hard-won independence, had been achieved through no lack of heartache. Did he really imagine that on a whim he could just walk back into their lives?

'You'll want to see Gemma. We can arrange times now,' she replied effortlessly.

'And I want to see you, Ali,' he interrupted her sharply. He moved towards her, large palms held upward in a gesture of entreaty. 'Don't shut me out, Alison. Please. I want to do…what's best…for all of us.'

'What *was* best for Gemma and I,' Ali countered before she could stop herself, 'was to be a family, Sam. But you rejected that. You made your choice—and it has nothing to do with me if it didn't work out. I've no objection to you seeing Gemma—but, please, don't try to interfere in our lives.'

With that she turned and walked to the staircase, ascending it with legs that didn't seem to be part of her anatomy, aware he was staring after her. But she didn't look back. And when she entered her room and sat quietly in her chair, she knew the first hurdle was over.

It was a small achievement. But it was vital. Vital to her self-esteem and to her confidence. Whatever Sam had to say, it could never alter the fact that he had betrayed her and thrown away their chance of happiness.

Eila Hayward, looking far younger than her twenty-five years with her large and expressive eyes, breathed in and out slowly, allowing herself a smile as Alison listened to the baby's healthy heartbeat. 'It's a boy,' Eila said confidently as she eased herself into a comfortable position on the couch. 'Mark said it was from the word go.'

Alison smiled curiously as she removed the stethoscope and began to take her patient's blood pressure. 'Why is your husband so certain?'

'Well, for a start, he's papered the nursery in blue.'

'Is he really that keen to have a boy?' Alison wrapped the cuff around the top of Eila's arm, slightly concerned at what she had just been told.

'Absolutely. Oh, he says he won't mind if it's a girl, but I know secretly he'd be devastated, him being so football mad. That's why I chose not to find out before the birth. After all, we can't send it back, can we?'

Alison hadn't realised her patient was fretting about the sex of her baby. For the five months she had been treating Eila Hayward, the young woman hadn't referred to the sex of the child. That this should be revealed today, in Eila's last month of pregnancy, was a surprise.

'In my experience,' Alison said, as supportively as she could, 'most new fathers are overjoyed at whatever arrives, especially if they're there at the birth. It's an illuminating experience for any man.'

Eila nodded slowly. 'Have you any children, Dr Stewart?'

'Yes, a daughter. She's twenty-two months.'

'Did your husband attend the birth?'

'Yes…yes, he did.'

'Was it a good experience for him?'

Alison helped her patient to her feet, then returned to her desk. 'My husband's a doctor, so he was well aware of what was about to happen.'

Eila Hayward stared at her. 'You don't mean *the* Dr Stewart who joined the practice last week?'

Alison staunchly fixed her eyes on the records she was updating. 'Yes, that's right.'

For a moment there was silence, then her patient sank into the chair beside the desk. 'I wondered if there was a connection.' She tilted her head thoughtfully to one side. 'I've often wondered what it must be like to work alongside your husband. If it were me, I'd get on Mark's nerves or he'd get on mine! Sometimes living together is bad enough—I mean, you know, it's the little things that irritate, isn't it? How on earth do you cope when you get home?'

'My husband and I are separated,' Alison said quickly.

'Oh, dear, I'm sorry,' Eila mumbled. 'Trust me to put my foot in it.'

'You didn't,' Alison assured her patient. 'Now, back to the baby—you're booked into Kennet General for the birth and I don't foresee any problems. Your BP is fine and you're in good health. I'm sure everything will go well.'

Eila smiled nervously. 'Thanks, Dr Stewart. Fingers crossed, eh?'

'You'll be fine,' Alison said encouragingly. 'Not long to go now.'

'I'll get Mark to drive me over a few bumpy roads.' Eila laughed as she walked into the hall. 'That should do the trick. Bye, Dr Stewart.'

After the young woman had gone, Alison closed the door and returned to her desk. She had managed to hide her emotions, she hoped, when talking about Sam and the birth of Gemma. Eila would have been surprised to know that Sam, too, had leaned towards a son. But the moment he had set eyes on Gemma, nothing had mattered except that she was healthy. He'd held her in his arms, fascinated, running tender fingers over her porcelain-like soft skin. It had been love at first sight.

Alison pulled herself sharply back to the present, the piercing ache inside her informing her that once again she had broken the rules she had set herself and slipped back to the past. Eila's comments had exposed a nerve and Alison knew she would spend the rest of the day paying for it.

Coupled with the fact she had to prepare to see Sam again, Eila's remarks did nothing for

Alison's composure. Nevertheless, she saw all her patients by one and managed to avoid the staffroom at lunchtime, eating sandwiches in her room. Her afternoon surgery went without a hitch, but it was at half past four that she glanced anxiously at her watch.

'All done,' Pam Shearing told her as she looked round the door. Pam's friendly, homely face broke into a smile. 'Unless you'd like to take the overspill? Dr Trenchard and Dr Stewart have both been called out.'

'All right,' Alison agreed. 'But I'd like to leave by five thirty, Pam.'

'I don't know what we'd do if it wasn't for your surgeries on Mondays and Fridays. No chance of adding another day, I suppose?'

'Sorry, Pam. I'm at Northreach Surgery on Tuesdays and Kennet on Wednesdays. Thursday is my only weekday with Gemma.'

'I know,' Pam agreed, laying the next patient's records on her desk. 'It's awkward, juggling home and work.' She laughed. 'You shouldn't be so popular, you know.'

'Flattery won't get you anywhere.' Alison grinned. 'But it was a good try.'

Pam raised her eyebrows and sighed. 'Still, with Dr Stewart coming back, it'll be much easier—' She stopped, looking embarrassed.

At once Alison assumed her mask. 'Yes, I'm sure. OK, Pam, let's have the next one in.'

Giving Alison a brief, apologetic smile, the dumpy, middle-aged receptionist quickly withdrew.

Another hurdle over, Alison thought with relief. She was about to look at the records in front of her when the door opened again. Instead of a patient, the tall figure of Sam entered. 'About tonight, Ali—' he began, but she was already standing up, her heart pounding as he strode toward her.

'I collect Gemma from Clare at around quarter to six—I'll be home shortly afterward,' she said in a clipped tone that brought him to a grinding halt.

'So, I can call? That's no problem?'

'No.'

He looked relieved. 'Ali, that's great. I—'

'Sam, you're Gemma's father,' she interrupted him quickly. 'I told you earlier that I'm happy for you to see her but, please, don't take it as an open invitation to step back into our lives.' Alison pulled herself up, for once grateful for her height. Her long-limbed body had been a source of embarrassment to her as a child when growing up faster and taller than all her friends. But when she had met Sam, who stood at a disarming six feet four, she had complemented his height perfectly.

He looked at her for a long time before answering, then slowly nodded, the muscle in his jaw working as he, too, stiffened his shoulders. 'Point taken,' he answered briefly. 'I shan't make a nuisance of myself. However, ten months—for me—has been a long time.'

'And for Gemma. She hasn't forgotten you. I've kept your memory alive, Sam. She needed that.'

She knew her words struck home, but so they should. It had been he who'd decided to go to Australia. He who'd decided to put his career first and consign his family ties to the past.

She watched him move slowly and heavily across the floor. At the door he paused and she waited, breath held, knowing every inch of him so well, recalling the gesture that would forever be Sam—a hand drawn slowly across his jaw, dropping heavily to one side.

Glancing at her with dark, hooded brown eyes, she gained no satisfaction from the pain she saw hidden in their depths. As the door closed behind him Alison sank down on her seat—utterly drained.

CHAPTER TWO

HECTOR TRENCHARD, at fifty-eight, was still a striking man. His black hair was peppered with grey now, but his blue eyes remained bright and humorous. Alison liked and admired Hector, the founder partner of Lamstone Surgery. He had never married, despite his many well-documented female friendships, but was broad-shouldered enough to take the ribbing that his staff and friends frequently showered on him.

Sam had joined him four years ago—'Turning over a new leaf,' Hector had laconically termed the practice make-over. But Sam had approached his new partnership with a natural zest which had uniquely transformed the surgery and overjoyed Hector.

But it wasn't of the early days that Alison was thinking as she joined Hector that evening on her way to the car park. Her mind was fully engaged on the present—in short, Sam's visit to see Gemma that evening.

'How did it go today?' Hector asked, apparently sensing her mood. The towpath bordered the river and the late sun was dipping into the willows dappling the water with silvery stars.

'Pretty well.' Alison attempted nonchalance. It was, after all, Hector who had suggested she take Sam's place and ironically it was he who had informed her of his return. 'To be fair, there wasn't much time to talk. Sam's seeing Gem this evening...' Her voice trailed off and Hector nodded pensively.

'His chief aim, I feel, was not to hassle you.'

Alison bit her lip. 'I'm afraid I find that difficult to believe, Hector.'

'Long-distance phone calls,' Hector replied in Sam's defence as they reached the car park, 'are never very satisfactory. And, to be fair, he only decided to return to England last month.'

'I don't doubt it,' Alison replied shortly. 'But I think I deserve to be informed, don't you?'

'It was entirely my suggestion that I act as go-between—'

'There's no need to apologise, Hector. It's not your fault. I know you think the world of Sam.'

'And of you, Alison.'

'Yes,' she agreed contritely. 'And it's reciprocated. It's just that Sam and I aren't together any more. We lead separate lives. And just because Sam—on a whim—decides to leave Australia and return to Britain...'

'That's the way it appears,' Hector cut in hesitantly, 'but I'm sure Sam gave the matter some serious thought.' He patted Alison's hand. 'However, I know you must feel apprehensive of his...er...motives.'

Threatened was probably a more accurate word, Alison thought but didn't say. Even though she had made her feelings crystal clear to Sam earlier today, she still felt deeply unsettled.

Alison had faced the fact that Sam had decided to make his life on the other side of the planet. She hadn't been concerned for herself, having finally come to terms with their separation. But it was Gemma who would suffer the consequences of an absent father. She had hoped they could be civilised about it—take Gemma's welfare into consideration before their own. Obviously Sam hadn't felt the same way. Once again he had placed his career first.

'Look, you need time to adjust,' Hector was saying gently. 'If after...say...a month, you've any qualms, then we'll think again. You could perhaps cover Sam's day off—or swap to Saturday mornings and weekend cover.

Whatever it takes, Ali, to keep you here. I don't want to lose you.'

Alison met his truly anxious gaze. 'I'm sure Sam and I will get on—once we establish a few ground rules.'

Hector gave one of his most charming grins. 'That's the spirit, Ali. Now, I must let you go.'

As she drove off, Alison was fully aware she had just encountered some of Hector's lethally persuasive tactics, though this time on behalf of Sam. It was always difficult to refuse Hector. Like the time he had offered her a partnership after Sam had left. For days he had waged a subtle battle to win her agreement. But being a single parent had changed her priorities and Gemma came first every time. A full-time career had been totally unrealistic.

Three miles on from Lamstone, Alison drove into Timpton village where Clare and her husband Robbie ran a market garden. The family home overlooked the business and Clare, in jeans and T-shirt, stood at the gate with Gemma in her arms, waiting for Alison's arrival.

Alison and Clare were soon chatting and for a while the cares of the day were forgotten. But eventually Alison glanced at her watch. 'Sorry, Clare, I must dash. As I said when I phoned you this afternoon, I'll have to take a rain check on supper.'

'No problem.' Clare shrugged easily. 'She's all bathed and fed, so you won't have much to do before Sam arrives.'

Alison strapped Gemma into her safety seat in the back of the car and hurriedly closed the door. 'He didn't say what time he was coming,' she murmured distractedly as she climbed in behind the wheel.

'Let me know how it goes.'

'I'll ring you after he's gone. OK?'

'Brilliant. Oh—she's dry, by the way. No accidents at all today.'

Alison gasped, wishing she had time to stop and talk. 'Really?'

Clare laughed. 'You'll be late if we start chatting. Speak to you later. And, Ali?'

'Yes?'

'Good luck tonight.'

Alison turned the key in the ignition sighing. 'Yes, something tells me I'll need it.'

Clare leaned in and kissed Alison on the cheek. 'Go home and have that shower.'

From the back seat Gemma squealed as her aunt made a funny face and waved goodbye. As Alison drove away, she glanced at Gemma in the rear-view mirror. Her heart squeezed

fiercely as Gemma's small blonde head lolled
sleepily to one side, her smooth lids closing
over her large brown eyes.

It was at times like this she felt dreadful
about leaving her. Shouldn't she have been
there to witness Gemma's first dry day? These
were occasions of special meaning, never-to-
be forgotten events. Yet she had been at work,
her attention divided between her patients
and—today—Sam in the room beneath hers.

How would she react when she saw him tonight? How would it feel to have his presence
under the roof of Keys Cottage again?

She soon turned into Keys Close, the narrow
cul-de-sac that carved a niche into ripe green
fields and corn meadows. Keys Cottage,
lemon-shuttered and lattice-windowed, stood a
convenient ten-minute walk from Clare's
house, fifteen minutes' drive from Lamstone
and was within a leisurely day's outing to
Oxford. Keys Cottage had been home to the
Stewarts for the past four years, and Alison
adored it.

She could clearly recall the day she and Sam
had chosen it. The look of surprise on the es-
tate agent's face when they'd said yes together
immediately when they'd opened the front
door.

She also recalled their first night—their love-drenched bodies curled on the futon upstairs, the only piece of soft furnishing in the whole house. The owl that had determinedly hooted from the copse each evening, the clink of batwing against glass. And then later, Gemma's soft mewing as she'd lain in her cot, winning Sam's undivided attention for the first few weeks. The sound of bare feet padding over boards in the middle of the night and hushed crying as he rocked her in his arms.

And sometimes, with an effort of will, she could even block out the heartache that followed. But only sometimes. On rare occasions when blissful, total exhaustion replaced that relentless agony of regret.

Sam stood at the cottage door, his dark eyes warily flicking over her shoulder to the hall beyond. 'Am I too early or…or too late?'

Alison's cheeks were flushed, her blonde hair looped up into a ponytail. To her shame she still wore the blue linen suit she had dressed in that morning for work. Abandoning the idea of a shower as Gemma had craved attention, she had made a feeble promise to herself to at least throw on clean jeans and a T-shirt. A touch of lipstick, a whisper of perfume and she would do. But even this had proved impossible as Gemma had seated herself in Alison's lap in the nursery and refused to move.

Sam, on the other hand, looked immaculate. Showered and changed into light-coloured chinos and a short-sleeved sports shirt open at the neck, his dark hair was damply combed back from his tanned features, not a hair out of place. And although his smile was hesitant, the flash of white teeth initiated the same old twist in her tummy that she found hard to ignore. Then there was the cologne, a tangy, pulse-racing scent that hadn't changed in all the years she had known him—and still had the desired effect.

Alison heard herself inviting him in, wretchedly self-conscious about her crumpled suit and her estranged husband's heart-stopping appearance. She motioned upstairs, to Gemma's nursery. 'We've been playing with the building bricks...' she excused herself lamely.

'The big, shiny, coloured ones?' Sam asked at once, apparently looking through her.

'The ones she couldn't even hold properly...' A sudden energy filled his voice and his eyes travelled yearningly up the stairs.

'Yes, the ones you bought her...'

'That's…nice…' he murmured, clearing his throat, and Alison felt as though she were falling—very fast—from a very high place. They stood silently, awkwardly as Gemma's little voice echoed.

He glanced at the safety devices fitted at the bottom and top of the stairs. 'She wasn't walking properly when I left…'

'No, she started the week after. Remember—the letter I wrote?'

He nodded slowly, his face averted. 'Can I go up?'

'Yes… I'll bring a drink…'

She watched him lift his long legs easily over the gate and lope up the stairs. Her heart banging frantically, she went to the kitchen and made coffee, slowing her movements deliberately. Her imagination portrayed the scene upstairs, his arms going around Gemma, lifting her, his cheek against hers, the soft baby mouth curling into a smile…an embrace that would have broken her heart to watch…

Suddenly there was a wail loud enough to wake the dead.

Alison almost dropped the coffee-pot. She raced from the kitchen, lifted her skirt and hurdled the stairgate. The second she flew over, just as Gemma let out another wail that sent shivers racing down Alison's spine.

When she reached the nursery, Sam was standing, almost paralysed, against the wall. Gemma was staring malevolently up at him, two large tears erupting from her eyes. Her little figure was dwarfed by Sam, one fist bunched around a building block.

'She...she doesn't recognise me!' Sam wailed. 'I'm frightening her, Ali—I'm a stranger!'

Alison was shocked. Surely Gemma recalled Sam! It hadn't even occurred to her that she wouldn't.

Alison rushed to pick up Gemma. 'It's all right, darling, it's Daddy—'

Gemma wailed even louder. Alison hugged her then looked at Sam. He was still frozen to the wall. 'For goodness' sake, don't stand there like that, Sam!'

'What shall I do?'

'I...I don't know. Move or something. Act naturally.'

'I'll go downstairs...' He peeled his large body away from the wall, colliding with a butterfly mobile as he did so. As he reached the door, Gemma shrieked all the more, her tears plopping onto her fat little arms.

'What's the matter, Gem?' Alison was beginning to panic. 'Gemma, this isn't like you...'

Her screams by now were deafening. Alison felt Gemma's little fists beat on her shoulders. The building block narrowly missed her face. It was then penny dropped.

'Sam, come back—please!' she called after him.

He peered round the door. Alison almost laughed. He looked like a rabbit caught in the glare of headlights. Gemma's screams ranged up to ear-piecing.

'I'm only making her worse,' mouthed Sam, disappearing again.

'Sam...you don't understand!' Alison hurried after him, struggling to hold on to Gemma.

In the hall, she found him sheltering by the potted palm. 'I'll go!' he protested as Gemma glared at him, tears streaming down her cheeks.

'You don't have to,' Alison called, laughing now.

'What's so funny?' Sam bleated.

''It's not you, Sam, it's what you have in your hand. The red brick with the duck on it. She must have thought you were taking it.'

He stared at the offending article clenched tightly in his palm. 'I didn't realise I was holding one,' he muttered, holding it out.

Gemma's sobs stopped instantly.

'Gemma—I'm so sorry, sweetheart,' he breathed softly as he moved towards her.

'Thank you, Daddy,' Alison said, urging Gemma to say the words as she grabbed the brick.

Gemma babbled, turning her head coyly.

'That was her version.' Alison grinned.

Kicking her dungareed legs, Gemma indicated the floor. Alison lowered her and she toddled into the nursery.

Sam stood, still in shock. 'Is she all right, do you think?'

'She's in better shape than you,' Alison grinned. 'I'm afraid she's very possessive about those bricks.'

Sam followed her. 'I suppose I should be flattered.'

At Gemma's door, Alison turned round. 'Yes, she's very fond of them. We play each evening when I come home. ''Daddy's bricks'', she calls them.'

'She really says that?' Sam asked as he cautiously looked round the nursery door.

'In her own fashion, yes.'

Gemma looked up at them and smiled contentedly. Alison always thought she looked like an angel at play, her curly white-blonde hair and peachy skin so unbelievably beautiful.

Sam gazed at his daughter, entranced. Gemma's bright smile extended to laughter and in a few seconds Sam had folded his long legs beneath him and was sitting on the floor beside her. Two large male hands reached out to balance one brick, extremely carefully, on another. A smaller pair of pink ones knocked them down.

There were gales of laughter.

Alison perched on the single divan—and watched.

'Does she sleep through the night?' Sam's deep voice was a whisper as they stood at the door of the nursery. The soft pink glow of the lamp beside her bed reflected on Gemma's sleeping form. Curled under the Snow White coverlet, her blonde curls fanned out over the pillow.

'Unless she has a…dream…yes.' Alison hesitated.

'She wakes when she dreams?'

'Sometimes. Then she'll come into our—my room,' she corrected herself quickly, 'and climb in beside me.'

Sam stepped back as Alison drew the door to, leaving a safe two-inch gap so if she woke, Alison would hear her. 'You mean, she has nightmares?' His face was full of concern.

'No, not exactly nightmares…she's too young, I think. Just…disturbances…' Alison led the way along the hall, not wanting to meet Sam's gaze. The dreams had begun after he'd left last year and were obviously related to his departure.

'Why didn't you tell me?' Sam asked as Alison unlocked the safety catch on the gate and let herself and Sam onto the staircase.

'What good would it have done?'

Sam held her arm. 'Ali, I want to know these things—'

'From three thousand miles away?'

'From any distance. She's my daughter.'

Alison freed herself from his grasp. 'Did you really imagine that leaving Gemma would be without its repercussions?' She headed down the stairs through the gate at the bottom and waited in the hall. Now that Gemma was asleep, there was nothing, in theory, left for them to discuss.

'Do you want me to go?' he asked as he reached the front door and saw her waiting.

Alison gave a grim little smile. 'What else is left to discuss, Sam?'

His dark eyes met hers. 'You and I?'

She took a long breath. 'Sam, you're welcome to see Gemma whenever you want. I'm placing no restrictions on you—you have after all ten months of absence to make up for. But there's nothing left for us to say.'

He looked at her gravely. 'Ali, don't be like this. OK, I know we haven't seen eye to eye about my return—'

'It wasn't your return as much as your leaving, Sam.'

'I thought it was best—at the time. I may have been wrong...'

'You thought it was best for you. Did you ever really consider seriously how it would have been for Gemma, growing up with a parent living on the other side of the world? Did you seriously consider what it would mean to her?'

'Ali, that's not fair.' His dark eyes were filled with emotion and Alison knew that, given a few moments more, she would be listening to him justifying the reason for him leaving for Australia and then, no doubt, ex-

cusing his affair. By some trick of nature she
would weaken, her defences would slowly
erode and all the effort she had put into sur-
viving without him would be wasted.

'Sam, I think it's time you went.'

'Why? Are you afraid to listen to what I
have to say?'

'I have listened—'

He stepped towards her and, reaching out,
caught hold of her arms. Staring down into her
face, he said very slowly, 'Not well enough,
Alison—evidently! I'll accept a portion of the
blame for our separation—and for the divorce
that you clearly intend to initiate. But I won't
take all the blame. That's unfair and unjust and
totally unrealistic. Now, either you and I discuss our future, without all these undercur-
rents, or you, Alison, must take full responsibility for what happens from now on.'

His outburst so shocked her that for one moment she was unable to reply, and it wasn't
until he had released her and was striding to
the door that she realised he was leaving.
Without casting her a backward glance, he let
himself out and Alison stared at the cottage
door which, left open, slowly closed and
clicked shut.

She heard an engine start up and it was this that caused her to hurry to the door and pull it open. The sleek blue car was halfway down the cul-de-sac. And if Sam saw her standing there, he gave her no indication of slowing.

Her cheeks burning, she stepped out onto the path, glaring after the car. Had he dared to accuse *her* of ruining their marriage?

Alison walked back inside, anger bubbling inside her. She had done everything she could to make it easy for him to see Gemma. What right did he have to come here tonight and lecture her on their future when only months ago he had shamelessly disregarded it himself?

After her longed-for shower, Alison carried the cordless phone into the garden and sat in the deckchair. It was a beautiful evening, the honeysuckle growing over the cottage wall deeply scenting the air. She loved the small country garden for its wildness and colour and the ease of maintaining the minuscule lawn bordered with flowers. The intercom was placed above the French doors and so she could relax, knowing she would hear Gemma if she woke.

Dialling Clare's number, Alison trailed her now calm fingers through her damp hair, grateful for the soothing effect of the cool shower and the soft cotton sarong. Sam's accusations had slightly receded from mind.

It was Robbie who answered in his usual cheerful fashion and Alison talked to him for a few moments. When Clare took the phone, she listened silently as Alison explained what had happened.

'Oh, dear,' Clare answered when she had finished. 'Was Sam right?'

'What do you mean?' Alison replied, disappointed that Clare hadn't commiserated.

There was a brief pause before her sister answered. 'Were you afraid to listen to what he had to say, Ali?'

'I *have* listened!' Alison retorted, shocked. 'It was Sam who didn't listen to me. Remember? After Gemma was born—'

'After Gemma was born, you were depressed, Ali.'

'Are you saying it was my fault he had an affair?' Alison demanded.

'No. I'm saying you weren't your usual self. Postnatal depression is just as much of a curse as a broken arm or leg, it's just that people don't see it. And I don't think Sam understood...'

'I tried to explain Ali—for heaven's sake, he's a doctor, he should understand!'

'Doctor's aren't infallible. Sam was working so hard and with all those broken nights—'

'Yes, according to Sam he was working,' Alison cut in bitterly.

'It was just one night Ali. I know it's no excuse but—'

'What would you think if Robbie was out *all* night—with another woman?' Alison demanded and held her breath, hating to say those words again, hating the very thought of it. Why was Clare making this conversation so difficult?

'I'd want to know why—of course. But knowing Robbie as I do, there would be a reason. And I'd have to decide if that reason was valid,' Clare replied levelly, but Alison felt herself snapping back.

'That's because Robbie is Robbie. He's utterly faithful, Clare.'

'Which is all the more reason—if he strayed—for me to understand why he did.'

Clare's meaning wasn't lost on Alison. It had always been Clare's and Alison's understanding that both Robbie and Sam were faithful husbands, so unlike their father. Even now after all these years, Alison couldn't believe that her own father had walked out on their mother for a younger woman.

'Ali—are you still there?'

Alison swallowed. 'I'm here.'

'Look, I'm not taking Sam's side. I'm just saying…you weren't yourself. Heck, what do I know about it? You're the doctor. But post-natal depression is so debilitating, Ali. For those around you, too, who can do nothing to help.'

The lump in Alison's throat expanded as the memories she kept determinedly buried came flooding back. She didn't want to be reminded of the depression that had struck without warning and which she had felt so guilty about.

It was Clare who then discreetly changed the subject, and when Alison had said good-bye, she sank back in the deckchair, staring at the phone. What Clare had said held the ring of truth.

With a sinking feeling, Alison confronted herself with the internal dialogue that always left her with yet more questions than she had answers.

What was she really afraid of? Was she too proud to accept that postnatal depression had deeply affected her judgement—albeit tempo-rarily? Had the depression she had suffered forced Sam away from her?

Just then the intercom sounded and Gemma's call pierced the night air. Alison hurried inside and went up to the nursery. Gemma was sitting up in bed and rubbing her eyes. Alison enfolded the hot little body into her arms, wishing inexplicably that Sam was here to comfort her.

Northreach Surgery was Alison's destination the following morning. After leaving Gemma at Clare's, she drove the eighteen miles through the country lanes towards Cirencester to Dr Christine Morgan's village practice, where she acted as locum.

Sadly, the surgery was to close at the end of the year and Alison had been approached by the retiring GP to help in the winding down of her rural practice.

Alison's day at Northreach always proved cathartic. Christine had a sense of humour second to none and philosophically accepted the demise of her surgery. Animal farming was disappearing. Alternative lifestyles and commuting to the towns were favoured by the new generation—a fact emphasised by the lack of old and battered vehicles that had once lined the grass verges outside the converted farmhouse.

Alison was witness to a new breed of country life. Smart four-wheel-drive vehicles and hatchbacks that looked as if they had emerged from the pages of a glossy magazine now swooped down the country lanes. Drivers sported designer wear and laptops, rather than tweed jackets and gumboots.

'The end of an era,' Christine Morgan had been heard to remind her dwindling patients. 'So make the most of me whilst you can.'

'We've got one vertigo, one glaucoma—you remember Ted Stockton last week—and four miscellaneous,' Jenny Wilkins, the receptionist-cum-jack of all trades, told Alison when she arrived. 'Dr Christine's gone out on a delivery—a calf. The vet's down with flu.'

This was what Alison loved about Northreach. She had learned to expect the unexpected. The fact that the intrepid lady doctor was deputising for the vet didn't surprise her in the least. Moreover, Jenny Wilkins, who had worked at the surgery for three decades, also knew every patient on the Northreach list. Diagnosis was frequently arrived at over the telephone, even before the patient set foot in the surgery. So Alison was surprised when she added hesitantly, 'Oh, yes, and someone rang for you—a doctor. Said he'd call later on.'

'Who was it, Jenny?' Alison called as she was halfway down the hall.

'Didn't catch the name. Bad line.'

'If he calls again, put him through. It's probably Hector Trenchard.' Guessing that Hector remained concerned about her and was still attempting to smooth troubled waters, Alison smiled to herself as she walked the narrow, slightly shabby-looking hall to the smallest room on the ground floor. Full marks to Hector for trying.

Alison opened the door to her room and was zapped by the bracing scent of one of Jenny's lavender air-fresheners. At least there was a clear pathway to the desk. Alison was eternally grateful that she had insisted on a junk-free zone since starting at Northreach.

At her request, Jenny had reluctantly removed a cupboard overflowing with boxes and endless piles of ancient magazines. The post-war desk and examination couch, however, were in reasonable condition and had, with a good polish, proved invaluable.

As she sat at the desk and glanced at the handwritten list and dishevelled pile of records on the top of it, Alison smiled once more. One vertigo, as diagnosed by the elderly patient himself—a note on top in Jenny's handwriting to explain. Ted Stockton, a retired farmer with glaucoma, complete with hospital records. Four other 'miscellaneous', as Jenny had described them.

Ten minutes later Alison was hard at work, listening to the elderly farmer recording the catastrophes caused by his failing eyesight. By midday she had seen all six appointed patients and was well into her list of late callers.

Christine Morgan arrived back from the calving with a smile all over her plump, weatherbeaten face. Alison ended her day at Northreach, as usual, in a far better frame of mind than she had reached it. Halfway home however, her mobile rang. Recalling she had forgotten to take it into the surgery with her, Alison pulled off the road to remove it from the dashboard compartment.

'Alison—it's Clare.'

The first sense of trouble came as Alison heard Clare's slightly breathy tone. 'There's no panic, but Robbie caught himself on some glass this morning.'

Alison sat up in her seat. 'What happened, Clare?'

'Some kids lobbed stones at one of the greenhouses. Robbie tried to mend it but in doing so cut his leg rather badly. He's all right, but we had to go to Casualty.'

'Oh, God, Clare—'

'I tried your mobile. Were you switched off?'

'Yes, I left it in the car.' Alison admitted, cross with herself.

'Well...the thing is...I...I let Sam take Gemma.'

'Sam! But why?'

'Ali, I didn't think I should take Gemma to the hospital with me. I had no idea how long they would keep Robbie. And since I couldn't get hold of you, it seemed the best place for Gemma to be was with her father.'

'Where are they now?' Alison asked anxiously.

'Sam's at the cottage,' Clare replied, 'so don't come here—go straight home.'

'Home...?' Alison repeated, trying to control the panic threatening to overwhelm her.

'Yes, I gave him my key—you don't mind, do you?'

Alison felt powerless to reply, her stomach forming itself into a knot, until somehow, realising that Clare must have been frantically worried about her husband, she pulled herself together. 'Of course not. Do you need any help with Robbie?'

'No, I'll ring as soon as I have any news.'

After Clare rang off, Alison sat where she was, trying to assemble her thoughts. Then, with a growing sense of foreboding, she drove home.

CHAPTER THREE

ALISON didn't know what she expected to find when she turned into Keys Close, but it certainly wasn't the peaceful vision of the cottage standing, as it did, on the curve of the cul-de-sac, cosseted by trees and burgeoning shrubs.

The only difference this evening was the pink light that already burned in Gemma's bedroom window, denoting the fact that someone had arrived there before her. Alison swallowed thickly as she parked behind the single foreign object in the road, Sam's car.

Tonight, the scent of honeysuckle went unnoticed as she fumbled for her key and thrust it into the lock. The door squeaked open, creaking on its hinge.

She held her breath and waited, the drumming of her heart obscuring other sounds. A trail of towels, shoes, dungarees, colouring books and a few scattered crayons led the way to the kitchen.

Alison hurried there, her blue eyes wide in apprehension, but as she entered, a lazy, peaceful feeling engulfed the room and a deli-

cious—if foreign—smell pervaded the air. She
stood at the pine table, her gaze slowly moving
to the Aga. One of the two ovens signalled it
was in use by the glow of a small ruby-red
light. On the hob, as yet uncooked, peeled car-
rots and potatoes had been placed in water-
filled saucepans.

As her heart settled back in to its normal
rhythm, she turned and retraced her steps.
Pausing at the bottom of the stairs, she listened
to the now audible hoots of laughter from the
bathroom—Sam's deep and throaty, Gemma's
delighted.

Alison allowed herself a further few minutes
to adjust. Returning home and finding the
house inhabited, Sam's presence dominating
what appeared to be bathtime and the startling
fact that supper was on the Aga, took some
getting used to.

The closer Alison got to the bathroom, the
clearer it became that Gemma was having a
ball. Bathtime was proceeding noisily and, by
the sound of it, very wetly. Her conclusions
were confirmed as she ascended the stairs,
hiked herself over the gate and pushed open
the bathroom door.

Sam was on his knees beside the bath, his
white T-shirt drenched, his dark hair flopping

boyishly over his face. He looked up at her with a broad smile that held no hint of surprise—or apology.

'Hi, there! Look, Gem, Mummy's home.'

Ignoring him, Alison bent down and kissed Gemma's wet cheek, catching as she did so the faint but intrusive whiff of Sam's cologne.

'Mum-um-um.' Gemma giggled, busy pouring bubbles into a plastic container and squashing them with her flannel.

'Why didn't you let me know what happened today?' Alison sank down on the bathroom stool and looked at Sam.

'I tried.' He shrugged casually as he tipped the contents of Gemma's little watering-can over her outstretched hands. 'Your mobile was off. And when I phoned Northreach I got some odd person talking about calves and cows.'

'Christine deputised for the vet—' She broke off as Sam arched a rueful eyebrow. Alison ignored it. 'What about work?' she countered quickly.

'My day off—luckily.'

Alison wondered why she felt so annoyed. Was it with herself for being unavailable when Clare and Gemma had needed her? Or was it with Sam for coping with the crisis so—apparently—competently?

'I could have driven the eighteen miles out there this morning to tell you,' Sam murmured dryly. 'But as I was off duty, it seemed hardly fair to worry you. And, as you can see, we seem to have survived the day intact.'

A fact Alison was forced to agree with as she watched Gemma splashing happily in the bath.

'Did Clare tell you what happened to Robbie?' Sam asked.

'Only that he hurt himself on glass from the greenhouse.'

'And some!' exclaimed Sam, whistling through his teeth. 'Clare rang me at about nine. Apparently you'd just left when Robbie came in, blood pouring from his leg. Clare patched him up, rang your mobile, then phoned the surgery and Hector rang me.'

'Why didn't she call an ambulance?'

'Robbie. He didn't want to make a fuss.'

'Men!' Alison groaned.

Sam looked at her with reproach.

'Da-a-da-, play!' Gemma heaved a plastic duck from the water and splashed it into Sam's submerged palm.

'Thank you, sweetheart, but duty calls.' He chuckled and, perching the duck on the side of the bath, stood up. 'It's Mummy's turn now.'

Alison was suddenly aware of his presence, of how much of the bathroom he seemed to take up as he replaced the towels on the rail. Her eyes flicked over the long lean back and jeans-clad legs and the swell of muscle on his tanned forearms as he replaced the top of the bubble bottle.

Alison turned quickly away. Had she managed to hide the rush of deep colour that had swept into her cheeks? What could she be thinking of!

Her life with Sam was firmly in the past—where it belonged. But coming home and finding him here had for a while disorientated her. It seemed like for ever that he was there, but a few minutes later he was whistling his way downstairs, which—only fractionally—served to restore her composure.

It was a warm June night and Alison stared out from the bedroom window, recalling the summer they had moved into the cottage. Sam had pruned the fruit trees vigorously. Now dark red plums were as sweet as sugar to taste and the smell was heady. It travelled into the cottage at night and was almost as potent by day.

Alison inhaled. In the fields beyond the garden a blanket of mist crawled closer. It would soon be dark and a little foggy, just as it had been that first night, four years ago...

She heard Sam downstairs and returned, with a jolt, to the present. Frowning at her reflection in the mirror, she asked herself why she had taken so much care with her appearance. Why shower at length, pamper herself with her favourite perfume and dry her hair—carefully—into soft blond waves? If she didn't still care, a voice whispered inside her head, if she didn't still feel something, would she have gone to such trouble?

'No,' she whispered, shaking her head determinedly. 'No more questions tonight. Just go down. Eat. Say goodnight. And count your blessings.'

Pulling back her shoulders under the soft blue silk blouse tied at the waist, which she had teamed with a flowered skirt, she checked on Gemma, then made her way downstairs.

'Gem OK?' Sam asked over his shoulder as she entered the kitchen. He was standing at the Aga, stirring the contents of a saucepan.

'Yes, she's asleep.' Alison pulled out a chair and sat down, feeling as though she were the unwilling participant in a game of time travel.

'Supper's nearly there,' Sam informed her, adding to her disquieting sensation of *déjà vu*. 'Chicken's sliced. Just waiting for the veg and roast potatoes.'

He had always been able to cook—brilliantly—a result of his student years and living in shared accommodation with three other males. Unlike Robbie, her lovable but utterly clueless brother-in-law, Sam was a dream in the kitchen.

Alison glanced away from the tall figure at the Aga. She didn't want to think of Sam's accomplished culinary skills which always led her down the road of the early years, the evenings they had spent, eating, laughing, making love, lying by the fire and talking afterwards...

She asked quickly, 'What did you do today?'

Sam chuckled softly as he stirred. 'You name it, we did it. Strolled by the river, fed the birds. Went to the market, trawled every stall. Ended up in the garden, pulling up weeds...or at least I hope they were.'

'Gemma wasn't tired after all that?' she asked, astonished.

He laughed again. 'We cheated. She rode on my shoulders most of the time.'

Alison nodded slowly. 'She always liked to, didn't she? Even when she was very small—before she could walk properly.'

It was then that he lowered the spoon and turned to look at her. His white T-shirt glowed against the tan of his skin and his dark brown eyes were sparkling—as they always used to when he wasn't tired, when work hadn't got the better of him and when they had salvaged a few precious hours together, to make love and forget the rest of the world. 'You remember that, too?' he asked softly.

She nodded and her eyes met his. The room took on an odd spinning sensation and it seemed an eternity before either of them spoke again.

'You look beautiful tonight, Ali,' he told her. 'That blue…what is it? Silk? It's the colour of your eyes.' He paused, leaning back against the worktop to stare at her. 'You know, in all the time I was away, that was the one thing I could remember clearly—your eyes,' he whispered so that she could barely hear him. 'I missed you—missed Gemma—more than I could ever have imagined possible…'

She felt herself weakening, her traitorous body trembling at his nearness, just the way it had trembled upstairs in the bathroom. She drew her hands together and clenched them, lifting her eyes slowly. Sex with Sam had always been heaven—a release, a joy, an addiction—and she could feel her body clamouring for him now.

'Then why leave, Sam?' she heard herself ask. This was uncharted territory. No tantrums, no sarcasm, no recriminations. Just a simple question.

'Because,' he murmured, 'at the time, it seemed the best thing to do.'

'The best thing...?' she repeated incredulously.

'We'd separated, Ali. You wanted a divorce—'

'We discussed the options,' she corrected swiftly, shocked at his twisting of events, 'and we both agreed that separating was the best for Gemma.'

'Ali, I didn't want a separation, much less a divorce. For God's sake, I loved you—and Gemma. You were my world.'

It was this remark that brought her to her senses. Did he really expect her to believe he loved her after what he had done?' Sam, I'll accept that you love Gem, that you missed her, but don't try to justify your...your actions...' She stopped, drawing herself up, unable to complete her sentence, the word 'affair' too painful to articulate. She swallowed, taking a sharp breath. 'You have your life now—I have mine. What you do now or with whom is no business of mine—any more than what I do is yours.'

He stared at her, the small muscle working in his jaw when he spoke. 'I don't recognise you, Alison. I don't understand you. I thought this evening we had made progress. But you've changed and I see no way of reaching you.'

'You weren't in that frame of mind,' Alison replied calmly, though inside she was shaking, 'when you left for Australia.'

She knew that she had probably gone too far, as he stared at her for a few minutes, then raised himself slowly from the worktop. 'I don't think there's any point in me staying to supper,' he muttered as he walked to the door and paused there. 'In view of what you have just said, I think we had better avoid situations like today which, although for my part they were well intentioned, only seem to distance us further. Goodnight, Alison. Give my love to Gem.'

She watched him leave, his footsteps light along the hall, the creak of the front door only serving to emphasise the stillness of the house after he had gone.

Alison stared at the space where he had been, her eyes filling with angry tears. She had fought her corner and clearly won. But winning an argument didn't alter the fact she could still smell him, see him, hear his voice as it dropped several notches to that deep, sensual rasp that always sent her tummy reeling. And she could still feel the band of pain that encircled her heart at his final words.

Slowly she rose and went upstairs and, despite the open windows in each room, the warm summer night seemed even more humid. She went into Gemma's room and opened the window a few more inches, closing the insect netting over it and finally the curtains. Then she sat beside Gemma and stroked the blonde waves that spilled over the pillow.

'Daddy says goodnight, darling,' she whispered achingly.

Refusing to let the tears fall, Alison kissed her daughter and left the room, going downstairs once more to the empty kitchen. She switched off the Aga controls, unable to gaze at the food there. Instead, she went into the garden and sat in the deckchair, staring up into the heavenly night sky.

There had been a time when, even after the affair, she could have forgiven him, she told herself, swallowing determinedly on the obstruction in her throat.

But Australia had changed all that.

And, as Sam had observed, it had changed her, too.

The following morning, Wednesday, Clare rang as Alison left for work

'Robbie's OK,' she explained hurriedly. 'I can't think how he managed to cut himself so badly.'

'What—exactly—happened, Clare?'

'Oh, nothing to make a drama of. Robbie's as strong as an ox. However, like a lot of men, he collapses at the sight of his own blood. But Sam was fantastic. He managed to staunch the flow coming from Robbie's leg and made him elevate it until the ambulance arrived. Honestly, if it hadn't been for Sam taking over, my silly husband might have bled to death.'

'Sam's a doctor, Clare, he ought to know what he's doing,' Alison responded crisply.

'So things didn't go so well last night?' Clare guessed at once.

'Oh, Gemma was fine, but Sam and I…well, we had a few words.' Alison sighed, reluctant to elaborate. The last thing she felt like listening to was Clare singing Sam's praises. 'Clare, I'm running late, but is there anything I can do to help?' she asked quickly, eager to change the subject. 'Robbie won't be mobile for a day or two, will he?'

'I've telephoned Marge and she's coming in with her husband to help out for the rest of the week, bless them.' Alison knew Clare's retired neighbours. As keen gardeners, they often helped Robbie when he was short-staffed.

'Will you let me know how Robbie is?' Alison asked quickly, checking her watch whilst keeping one eye on Gemma who was sitting at her feet, investigating the contents of her bag.

'I'll ring tonight. Are you taking Gem with you?'

'Yes. But I'm only on duty at Kennet until two, so I'll take her to the park afterwards for a paddle.'

When she had finished speaking to Clare, Alison prepared to leave for Kennet Health Centre, a fifteen-minute drive from Timpton.

Kennet was a recent addition to her schedule. The large health centre offered a crèche facility, enabling her to take Gemma along. Alison had discovered a park close by, with a play area and paddling pool. The weather had held throughout May and June and Gemma looked forward to her weekly excursions.

Alison hurriedly packed the picnic which she had prepared, installed Gemma in her car seat and set off for Kennet. It was once again a beautiful summer's morning and as she drove through Lamstone, she couldn't help but glance at the towpath car park, where Sam's car would be parked.

The sight of it—although she was prepared—caused the inevitable loop-the-loop in her stomach. This wasn't helped by the sudden sight of Sam standing outside the surgery. He looked very tall and tanned, dressed in light trousers and a deep blue short-sleeved shirt. Apparently unaware of the passing traffic, he was in conversation with a young woman. Alison felt her eyes drawn inexorably to them and her heart went into what seemed like free-fall as she thought she recognised the small, dark-haired figure dressed all in white.

'Dad…da…dad…da,' cried Gemma, as she too saw Sam.

'I know, darling, it's Daddy,' Alison breathed, attempting to concentrate on the road yet needing desperately to look again.

When she managed a last glance they had both disappeared, and Alison looked back at the road, attempting to calm herself. It took the full fifteen minutes of her journey to Kennet to convince herself she had been mistaken in thinking she'd recognised the girl talking to Sam.

And by the time she had parked and entered the spacious reception area of the health centre, given Gemma over to the care of the child-minders and seated herself at her desk, Alison had almost decided that her imagination had been playing tricks.

With no extras attached to her list, it was just after two o'clock when the last of her patients left and Alison hurried to collect Gemma.

'Paddle!' Gemma demanded at once as Alison entered the bright room that housed the practice crèche and scooped Gemma up into her arms.

'Picnic first, darling. Then you can paddle.' Alison thanked the staff and, taking the buggy from the car, walked with Gemma along the tree-lined street that led to the park. Here the paddling pool was already full with other small visitors dressed in swimsuits and armbands.

Soon making friends, Gemma joined the group of splashing toddlers and Alison knelt at the side to watch. It was then, as Gemma played, that Charlotte Macdonald came back to mind, the practice nurse with whom Sam had had an affair.

Was she still a part of Sam's life? Alison wondered as she continued to stare at Gemma in the pool. And why should it bother her if she was? After all, she had told Sam only last night that his life was no concern of hers—so was that the truth or was she deluding herself as well as Sam?

The answer was, she realised, very simple. She wouldn't be sitting here now, thinking about Charlotte Macdonald, if she didn't care. And with a wave of dismay she found herself jolted back to the present—and the uncomfortable sensation that she had only been fooling herself whilst trying to convince Sam she didn't care.

CHAPTER FOUR

THURSDAY passed too swiftly as usual. It was Alison's free day and she enjoyed spending it with Gemma. This Thursday however, they spent shopping for Clare.

'I'll have Gemma tomorrow,' Clare offered bravely as Alison delivered the groceries. 'Robbie can't possibly have another accident, not two in one week.'

'And tempt providence?' Alison replied with a grin. 'No, I'm organised for tomorrow, Clare. Meg is quite happy to have Gem for the day.'

'Are you sure?' Clare asked doubtfully.

'Of course. Just make certain Robbie behaves himself.'

'I wish!' Clare waved them goodbye, and as Alison turned the car into the adjoining road, she made a mental note to put the alarm on for a half an hour earlier in the morning so that she could leave instructions with Meg before leaving.

Friday dawned with rain and lashings of it. Meg Holroyd, Alison's cleaning lady, arrived on the dot of eight.

'Meggee-ee,' Gemma squealed as the back door of the cottage opened and a small, grey-haired, bustling figure came in.

'Hello, poppet.' Meg grinned as she shook herself on the mat and greeted Gemma and Alison with a big smile.

'I hoped you'd be able to sit in the garden or go out for a walk,' Alison sighed as she hung Meg's soaked mac by the Aga and pulled on her own waterproof coat.

Meg merely shrugged as she lifted Gemma into her arms. 'We'll find lots to do, won't we, scamp?' She chuckled at Gemma.

'Here's all the relevant phone numbers if you want to reach me.' Alison grabbed the list she had made from the kitchen table. 'I'm at Lamstone all day, as you know, so I can be home in ten minutes. There's cold meat and salad in the fridge and ice cream in the freezer. She'll probably have a nap around two. Now…have I forgotten anything…?' Alison hesitated as she lifted her case.

'Not a thing.' Meg grinned as she shooed Alison out of the back door. 'Now, off you go and don't worry about a thing. Wave to Mummy, Gem.'

Alison's last glimpse of her daughter was as she dashed through the downpour to the car. Gemma waved happily, content to stay with Meg, as she had on many occasions before when Clare had been unavailable.

On her drive to work, experiencing the usual guilty pangs at leaving Gemma, Alison found herself thinking again how lucky she was. Gemma was outgoing and confident, even at twenty-two months. The separation had caused no visible signs of disturbance to her happy nature. And that was how Alison wanted it to stay.

As she turned into the car park, Alison peered up at Sam's room as she pulled on the handbrake. The light was on, as were most of the lights in the waterfront building. Was he looking out, aware of her arrival? And if so, after Tuesday's harsh words, what were his thoughts?

Alison took in a breath then opened the car door, preparing herself for both the rain and meeting Sam. In an instant she was drowned, despite pulling up her hood and fastening her coat.

In Reception, a queue of glistening raincoats lined up under the oak-beamed ceiling of the reception area. She smiled at Lucy and Pam, the two girls on duty at the desk, then, without pausing, hurried to the staircase, barely pausing to pull back her hood.

In her room, she breathed easily, uncertain whether her damp clothes or the disturbing thought of meeting Sam's large presence along the way had caused her to rush.

It was only after she had placed her coat on the back of a chair to dry that she noticed the piece of white paper, folded in two and propped against her computer. Disregarding it for the moment, she combed her damp blonde hair and brushed the scattered raindrops from her dark blue linen skirt.

When finally she sat at her desk and unfolded the paper, it read, 'Alison, after surgery—the ferry—if you can.'

She hadn't thought of the ferry in years— *their* place. Did it still exist? The Lamstone beauty spot was a landing stage on the river used by tourists for riverboat rides. On the far side, a sandy trail skirted fields of corn...a walk that she and Sam had made so many times...

Taking a long breath, she lifted the phone. 'Sam?'

'Hi.'

She paused, trying to guess at his mood. 'I read your note…'

'And?'

Her fingers tightened automatically at his abrupt tone. 'It's wet out there—or hadn't you noticed?'

'I noticed. We liked the rain once, remember?'

She swallowed, moistening her lips with her tongue. How could a few little words cause her to feel so threatened, so vulnerable? She said quickly, 'And I'm afraid I won't have time. Looking at my list—'

'We used to *make* time, Ali,' he cut in briskly. 'Just an hour—that's all we need. We have to sort this thing out. I think you know that.'

'Sam—'

'I'll be there. Join me—please.' The line went dead. Alison stared at the phone. She couldn't believe she had allowed this to happen. She wouldn't—couldn't go, not to that place. 'No,' she said aloud as she replaced the phone. If they were to talk, it couldn't be there. Too many memories, too many associations…

Where, then? A small voice inside her head asked. Aren't you running out of options?

'Anywhere,' she whispered, 'but not *there*.'

Alison jumped as the phone rang.

'Your first patient hasn't shown up,' Lucy told her quickly. 'Must be the rain. They're dropping off like flies.'

'Have you anyone waiting?' Alison asked, looking down at the list in front of her.

'No one as yet. And with this weather I wouldn't be surprised if more cancel anyway.'

An answer that, on this day of all days, Alison didn't want to hear.

The jetty, or what remained of it, poked out from the river bank, just visible under the mossy freefall of weed. The old clinker launch had long since disappeared and a notice planted on firmer ground stated that the land had been bought for development.

Having parked her car on the road, and with no sign of Sam, Alison stood listening to the silence. Her day had been short—thanks to the weather. There really had been no reason for her not to come—especially since the rain had stopped and a blue sky was peeping through the grey clouds.

Alison wrenched her eyes away from the river and all its memories. It was painful to return here. Surely he could have suggested somewhere else? Her large, soft blue eyes drifted slowly back, as though magnetically drawn, over the river's surface.

How many times had she and Sam caught the ferry to the other side and walked the path through the fields? It was impossible to say. The place was healing, addictively so. The earth always smelt wonderful, as it did today.

Alison reflected, not for the first time in her life, that this was the most beautiful place on earth.

'I shouldn't go any further,' a deep voice said, and for the second time that day, Alison started. She realised she'd been inching closer to the edge. 'The path's safer.' Sam's deep brown eyes stared penetratingly at her. Dressed in a navy sailing jacket with the collar turned up, his broad shoulders were hunched beneath, his hands pushed down into deep pockets. Alison swallowed at his heart-wrenchingly familiar presence.

'Why here?' she asked as she walked to the path.

'Why not?' His gaze held hers. 'We resolved all our problems here—once.'

Alison had to agree. However, their problems had been simple in those days.

'Shall we walk?' She spoke crisply, not wanting to dwell on either Sam's faithlessness or the agony his affair had caused. She must think of Gemma and what was best for her.

'Pity,' Sam murmured as they walked slowly together. 'The jetty's gone.'

'And so has the boat.'

'They're developing, by the looks of it.'

Alison nodded, hugging her arms around her as she walked. The air was cool after the rain and she shivered.

'So much for our walk in the rain.' He turned down the collar of his jacket and drew a hand over his thick dark hair. She could see the furrows in it where he had dragged his fingers through its thickness. His tan, she noticed, was a little less prominent now. But the distinctive features—the long, straight nose and achingly sensual mouth—seemed even more defined. She wondered, with a fresh stab of pain, if Charlotte Macdonald had been attracted to him in the same fierce way that she had…

'Thank you for coming,' he said, suddenly stopping. 'I thought talking—away from home or work—might help. Ali, I'd like to start afresh,' he added quickly, his eyes meeting hers for an instant. 'Since Tuesday I've had time to think and now I see you were right when you said our lives have changed. We've changed. We can't go back. The only way is forward. I realise we have to make this separation as painless as possible.'

Alison wondered why this statement didn't please her more. It was, after all, what she wanted. A painless separation. For Gemma's sake. Gemma adored her father, there was no doubt of that. And if it meant that she herself had to swallow her pride and hurt, then she would. Because Gemma meant the world to her. And whatever made her daughter happy also made Alison happy.

'So what do you suggest, Sam?' she asked, frowning.

'I thought,' he replied, stiffening at her abrupt tone, 'we might take Gemma out together occasionally. Attempt to keep up family outings. Acting the way we did on Tuesday seems rather pointless, given we both want what's best for her.'

Alison felt the knot in her stomach begin to unwind. 'When do you suggest the first of these outings?'

'I'm on call this weekend. Could you make the following Sunday?'

Alison nodded slowly. 'All right.'

'What time shall I collect you?'

Alison shook her head. 'Thanks, but we'll meet you there.'

'If that's what you want,' he replied abruptly.

They turned then and walked back in the direction they had come from, approaching the remains of the jetty. Neither of them referred to it as they passed and continued along the narrow path towards the road.

When their cars came into view, Alison ascended the grassy bank, only to stumble as her heels caught in the wet grass. She hadn't been expecting Sam's touch as his fingers gripped her arm. For a moment her body tensed as he steadied her.

'I thought you were about to fall.' His eyes met hers and it was all she could do to answer.

'I...I missed my footing,' she mumbled, disengaging herself from his strong grip and forcing her legs onward.

'See you on Sunday?' he asked as she unlocked her car and he came to stand beside it.

She nodded as she looked up from the driver's seat. 'Yes. I would like to make this work.'

'I hope we can, too.'

'I'd better go. Meg will be waiting.'

He was about to move away when he stopped. 'By the way, how's Robbie?'

'Oh, mending fast. You know Robbie.'

'Yes.' Sam grinned. 'He always was an irrepressible athlete.'

He stood for a few seconds more until finally she dragged her gaze away and said goodbye. She drove off quickly, refusing to allow herself to glance in the mirror.

She had managed to prevent herself from continuing the conversation. It would have been so easy. Just to talk about people and places they knew...in a life they had once lived...together. Her defences had weakened once. She wasn't about to let that happen again.

Over the following week there was little doubt in Alison's mind that Sam had decided to keep his distance. Though she saw him on Monday as she walked into surgery, he greeted her with a smile and a few brief words, but his first enquiry had been about Gemma. After that, though she saw him at odd times during the day, he made no effort to speak.

Her day at Northreach passed quickly and on Wednesday she made the journey to Kennet. As she passed the Lamstone practice on her way to take Gemma to Clare's, she recalled the previous week. The sight of Sam and the young girl standing on the steps outside had preoccupied her for some time. Had it really been Charlotte Macdonald? She wondered.

Since she hadn't seen Sam since Monday, Alison was able to concentrate on her schedule. Out of sight, out of mind, she decided. And because of this, Alison was apprehensive about meeting Sam on Friday. Despite his declaration that he intended to make their separation as painless as possible, could she take him at his word?

He was standing at Reception as she entered and he turned to say good morning. He was talking to Pam Shearing, one of Friday's reception team, and as usual Alison steeled herself as he smiled. When, she wondered, would she ever distance herself from those unhelpful pangs of yearning that came quite involuntarily as she saw him?

'Alison—have you a moment?' he called, turning briefly to hand some papers to Pam then striding over to her.

She was certain that he wanted to talk about Sunday and prepared herself to counter any questionable arrangement. She was surprised when this turned out not to be the case.

'A Thomas Knight—your patient—came in with his mother yesterday,' Sam told her. 'He had an asthma attack at school and the headmaster called his mother. She brought him in immediately, since his bronchodilator had no effect.'

Alison frowned as she recalled her fourteen-year-old patient. 'I'm sorry to hear that. Did he say what set the attack off?'

'Thomas thinks it was exercise-related. He was in the gym and using the ropes—and had to pull out. He told me his attacks are increasing.'

'Yes, the last one was in the early part of April. So what happened yesterday?'

Sam paused. 'He was in some distress, naturally...and somewhat embarrassed at having to use his medication in front of the class.'

Alison nodded, recalling that the teenager disliked using the inhaler. 'Did he use his bronchodilator here with more success?'

'No...I didn't urge him to do that. Instead, I went through a breathing technique—'

'A breathing technique?' Alison repeated, alarmed.

'Yes, Thomas seemed the perfect candidate for a form of asthma control I studied in Australia. I'd like him to continue with it, given your assent.'

'Sam, Thomas isn't a case to experiment with,' Alison replied in astonishment. 'He's been my patient since last November and his asthma can be extremely severe.'

'Which is why I think this technique will help,' Sam persisted. 'It's my belief that, with practice, Thomas will be able to decrease and finally cease the use of his bronchodilator.'

'You have no confirmed grounds on which to base that judgement.' Alison was angered at his arrogant statement. 'I've no intention of allowing Thomas to be used as a guinea-pig for some experimental idea that's still in its infancy and that I have absolutely no knowledge of.'

'Then let me explain—'

'The time to discuss it was before you saw Thomas and not after,' Alison broke in as her anger rose to the surface. 'Instead, you've probably added to Thomas's distress and confusion—which, when I saw him last, was a contributing factor to the problem of his asthma.'

'You're wrong, Alison,' Sam replied at once. 'Do you honestly think I would endanger a patient with some crank treatment that isn't tried and tested?'

'I've no idea,' Alison responded cuttingly. 'I fail to understand how your mind works as a man and, it appears, professionally. Now, if you'll excuse me, I have a full list to deal with.' She turned and walked quickly to the staircase, ascending it without glancing back.

In her room, she sat down at her desk and took a calming breath. Not only had Sam interfered in her private life but was now questioning her professional judgement. Changing Thomas's treatment without speaking to her first was totally unacceptable. Thomas was already alarmed by the intensity of these attacks; he certainly wasn't a candidate for a technique that Sam appeared to have latched onto.

After some thought, Alison lifted the phone and dialled Reception. 'Pam, before my first patient, please look up Thomas Knight's telephone number,' she asked. 'I'd like a word with his mother.'

'The boy who came in yesterday?' Pam said curiously. 'He was in rather a bad way, poor love.'

'Did you speak to Thomas?' Alison asked.

'No. I wasn't on duty when he came out. It was Dr Stewart, I think, who saw him. Do you want me to get Dr Stewart on his extension first?'

'No, I've already spoken to him,' Alison answered quickly. 'So, if you'll find that number for me, please?'

'Of course. I'll buzz you back.'

Whilst Alison took the few moments to deal with her anger, she wondered how she would approach Mrs Knight. Her concern was obvious, of course, but she didn't want to alarm the woman. And what if Thomas was home, still distressed with his asthma? Should she make a house visit? That depended, she supposed on Thomas's condition.

The phone rang and Alison picked it up quickly. 'The number you wanted is ringing,' Pam said, and after the familiar internal click of lines, Alison waited, her heart beating rapidly.

The number rang for some time until at last Alison replaced the receiver. She tried once more later that day and again before she left.

Was the telephone being deliberately ignored for some reason? she wondered anxiously.

Mrs Knight had mentioned she worked as a secretary and Mr Knight was the manager of a supermarket in Lamstone. There were two boys in the family—one younger than Thomas. It was a busy household—surely someone should be home at teatime?

Alison didn't see Sam as she left for home that evening. As she drove, her mind dwelt on Thomas who, with his former attacks of asthma, had twice been admitted to hospital. That his condition was severe was evident, yet Sam had blithely announced that a few breathing exercises would prove a cure!

Again her anger welled up and Alison decided that from now on both her professional and personal relationships with Sam were going to be conducted on a very different level.

A resolution which, in hindsight, Alison was to discover, lasted barely a day.

Gemma was tired and irritable on Friday when she collected her from Clare. Even Robbie who was now fully recovered and playing the clown, failed to rouse Gemma's interest. A cough kept her awake all night and by Saturday Alison feared that a cold was coming on.

However, it was worse than Alison had suspected as Gemma's temperature rose to thirty-eight centrigrade on Saturday evening. Gemma refused her supper, even when tempted her with her favourite ice cream.

By eight o'clock, it was clear she had a fever and her temperature was slowly rising. As Alison sat in the nursery with Gemma, the telephone rang.

'I'm just ringing to confirm the time for tomorrow,' Sam said before she could speak.

'Gemma isn't well,' Alison replied heavily. 'In fact, I'm quite worried about her.'

'What's wrong?' Sam asked, his tone anxious.

'Her temperature's raised and doesn't appear to be coming down. Besides which, she hasn't eaten all day, most unusual for Gem.'

'I'll come over,' he said at once, 'that is, if it's OK with you?'

There was no hesitation on Alison's part and she agreed immediately. All day she had tried to be objective, but she was finding it hard to be so. In the earlier part of the year, one of Hector's young patients had contracted meningitis and had it not been for Hector's swift diagnosis, the outcome wouldn't have been positive. Thankfully, the six-year-old had recovered.

Everyone at work had felt deep sympathy for the parents who had been frantic with worry. Even now, Alison could recall the fear on their faces as Hector had admitted their son to hospital. The threat of this life-threatening disease, contracted through a virus or bacterium, had touched them all, especially those with young children. And though Alison tried to rationalise her fears, as a mother she was the same as any other, worrying for her child.

Sam rang off and she hurried downstairs to unlock the front door. Ten minutes later, Alison heard it creak open and Sam's light spring up the stairs told her he had wasted no time in driving here. His face was full of concern as he entered the nursery and sat down on the edge of Gemma's bed.

'Hello, tinker, how's my best girl?' he said softly. Smiling briefly at Alison, he folded back the sheet. Gently pressing back Gemma's damp blonde hair, he bent to place a kiss on the top of her head.

Instead of her usual lively greeting, Gemma made no attempt to respond. Sam laid his hand on her forehead.

'How long has she been fevered?' he asked, turning to Alison.

'Since six—but she hasn't been herself since last night.'

'What have you given her?' he asked, the frown on his forehead deepening.

'Just paracetamol. She's due for another dose at ten.'

'And she's had no stomach pains or upsets? No vomiting?'

Alison shook her head. 'None at all. I thought at first it might be her teeth, but discounted that when her temperature soared.'

'Shall we just have a quick look, sweetheart?' Sam urged softly as he unclipped his case and took out a small torch. He looked at Gemma's throat, then checked her over fully, just as Alison had done several times earlier.

'Her glands aren't swollen and there's no spots or rashes,' he said finally. 'Perhaps sponging her down will help reduce the temperature.'

Alison nodded. 'Yes, I was about to do that when you rang.' As she left the room, Sam told her he would put on the fan. Alison found her eyes drawn to him as he reached up to the tall cupboards. Wearing a green and white sweatshirt tucked into the waistband of shorts, his long tanned legs ending in slip-ons, he looked entirely at home. How many times had she watched him make similar actions over the years they had been married, her eyes never failing to devour the sight of his long and powerful limbs?

The attraction she had always had for him had never diminished and as she cast her eyes away, she knew the chemistry was still there.

It was only when she reached the kitchen that she recalled why she had come downstairs—for Gemma's washing things. Taking a bowl and a freshly laundered Snoopy towel from the shelf, she went to the downstairs bathroom. It was here she tried to collect her thoughts as she found a sponge and flannel and poured lukewarm water into the bowl.

Suddenly she caught sight of her own reflection in the mirror—hurriedly scraped-back blonde hair, a few untidy wisps clinging around her ears, her soft grey shirt and multicoloured shorts looking somewhat rumpled.

But it was her deep blue eyes ringed by dark shadows that revealed her concern for the child that both she and Sam adored. And united in this love, Alison felt the closeness to him tug at her heart.

Stiffening her back, she tried to ignore the stab of pain that reminded her of the family life they had once shared. And because of this, or perhaps in spite of it, Alison knew that she wanted Sam beside her tonight.

CHAPTER FIVE

GEMMA finally fell asleep just before midnight. Curled under a thin cotton sheet and wearing only her vest, her blonde curls lay damply over the pillow.

Alison was making tea when Sam came into the kitchen. 'How is she?' Alison asked, turning to look at him as he drew out a chair and sat down.

'Still sleeping. But I'm not too struck on her temperature. I'd hoped the fan might bring it down.'

'I'll sleep on the futon tonight,' Alison said as she placed two mugs of tea on the kitchen table. 'It's still in the nursery.'

Sam took his mug and turned it thoughtfully, his eyes downcast. Then he looked at her. 'I'd like to stay—and be of help,' he added quickly. 'You look tired, Ali. Let me take the first shift.'

She took a gulp of her tea. 'Will you call me if she wakes?'

He nodded. 'With luck, she should sleep through. But if she doesn't, I'll let you know.'

Alison knew that his suggestion made sense, though whether or not she would sleep was another matter. She hadn't slept a wink last night, listening instinctively for Gemma, and she had been up several times to check her. Dawn had been breaking through the bedroom window as her eyes had closed finally, but she'd jumped out of bed almost at once as Gemma had let out a cry in her sleep.

Unable to return to bed, she had wandered round the house and finally showered and dressed. The day had passed slowly, probably, she realised, because Gemma's condition had deteriorated. And now, although she was still tuned in to Gemma, exhaustion was steadily creeping over her.

After drinking their tea, they went back upstairs, only to discover that Gemma was still very hot.

'I don't think I can sleep,' she sighed as she sank down on Gemma's bed.

'You will,' he told her quietly, 'if you try.'

'She's never been like this before Sam.'

'I dare say it won't be the last time.'

'It's just that I keep thinking…that there's something we're missing.'

'Doctors make the worst patients and the worst worriers,' he reminded her dryly. 'But we've both satisfied ourselves there's no rash…or stiff neck, which would indicate a more serious problem.'

Alison nodded slowly as she looked at Gemma. Sam was right. She mustn't let her imagination take hold. But this was the first time Gemma had ever had such a high temperature. Maybe she had just been lucky in the past—perhaps she had taken Gemma's good health for granted. She certainly wouldn't again.

She didn't resist when, after a few minutes, Sam gently urged her to her feet. In the light of Gemma's pink lamp, he cupped his hands on her shoulders and smiled. 'I'll check her every few minutes. Promise.'

'Sam, she's going to be all right, isn't she?'

'Of course she is. But you won't be, if you don't get some sleep.'

She was too tired to protest as he took her hand and led her to the bedroom. It was a large and elegant room with long oak beams traversing the ceiling. They had decorated it together and Alison hadn't had the heart to change anything in it since he had left. The wide double bed and its rattan headboard was where they had slept since that first night spent on the futon.

The terracotta pots spilling with dried flowers were her innovation, the handmade pine units and wardrobe were Sam's. The cream stone walls were decorated with sunny watercolours they had bought abroad, and most precious of all were her photographs of Gem.

As she stood with Sam she was thrown back years. They had been so happy here. What had happened to them? They had been a family once, a committed one. Or so she had thought.

'Get some rest now,' she heard Sam say beside her.

'Wake me,' she insisted as he pushed her gently down on the bed.

The hall light was on and she could clearly see his silhouette, though not his face. His outline was achingly familiar. It felt as though he had never been away. As though they were transported back to a time, when seeing him walking about the house in shorts and sweatshirt had been as normal as having him lie next to her, his nakedness next to hers, their bodies entwined both in love and in sleep.

Sex between them had always been good. Right back from the early days when she had first met him. Memories clamoured for release in her mind and she was unaware of lying back on the bed, her head sinking into the pillows.

Sleep soon overcame her. Her dreams were filled with Sam and Gemma. Bitter-sweet memories, filed away in her subconscious by day and set free to roam at night. Gemma in his arms, a few days old, his tall, muscular frame dwarfing his baby daughter.

Gemma in her pram, Sam bending over it...the cottage behind them...a pale blue sky beyond...then Sam coming towards her, as though she were taking a photograph. His laughter all around...his arms stretching out...and she, as always, desperate to go into them.

Yet somehow she couldn't.

Something, somewhere always held her back.

'Ali, Ali...wake up!'

The voice was Sam's, but she was sitting up even before he had finished his sentence. It was still dark and her mind told her there was something wrong. Sam wouldn't be calling her if there wasn't.

'Is it Gemma?'

'You'd better come.' His voice was gentle, attempting to stay casual. But she knew him too well. And with the instinct of a mother she also knew, as she stumbled along the hall, that Gemma had taken a turn for the worse.

It was just before dawn, when the world, even under normal circumstances, looked and felt less than reassuring, that Gemma's temperature soared. She began to twitch and jerk as Alison held her in her arms and tried to comfort her. Sam wasted no time in wrapping her up, bundling them all in the car and driving to hospital.

It was in Casualty that Gemma convulsed. As the emergency team surrounded her, Sam propelled Alison outside the cubicle.

The force of Sam's voice made her obey him as he pushed her down onto a chair. 'Alison, she's in good hands—we have to let them do their job.'

'But I'm a doctor, Sam—'

'We both are,' he reminded her sternly. 'But we're Gem's parents, too.'

'Sam...' Alison was distraught. For the first time in her life, Alison knew the meaning of terror. This was happening to Gemma. Her baby. Not someone else's this time, but hers.

After what seemed like an eternity, a nurse appeared. Alison jumped to her feet, her heart pounding so hard she couldn't speak. 'How is she?' she burst out, unable to contain herself.

'Your little girl is conscious now,' the nurse told them. 'The seizure was very brief and we're running some tests. Meanwhile, why don't you wait over here and I'll call you as soon as we know the results?'

'Oh, Sam, I can't believe this is happening,' Alison gulped as they followed the nurse to a cubicle. 'Why can't we see her?'

'It won't be long,' Sam whispered as he held her close. 'She's going to be all right. You must believe that. We both must.' The nurse left them in the privacy of the small room and Sam eased Alison down onto a chair. He sat beside her and murmured words of comfort. She held onto him, needing him more than she had ever needed him. Even their problems had no place in her thoughts right now. All she could think of was Gem.

'I'll get some tea,' Sam said after a while, but she shook her head.

'I don't want any,' she protested miserably. 'I just want to be with Gem.'

'Ali, I know how you feel,' he told her quietly, lifting a strand of blonde hair that had fallen over her face and tucking it behind her ear. 'I want to be with Gem, too. But they know what they're doing and we'll only be in the way. We just have to be patient, OK?'

Suddenly all her strength seemed to leave her. She nodded wearily. The last thing the casualty team wanted was the parents around at this critical moment, especially when those parents were doctors, too.

Sam went for tea and returned with two plastic cups full of hot brown liquid. It was strong and bitter, but Alison drank it gratefully.

'Better?' Sam asked, and she nodded.

'Sam…' she asked heavily, 'if the convulsion is triggered by an infection of the central nervous system…'

'The chances are that it's not,' Sam interrupted her quickly, reading her thoughts. 'Put meningitis out of your mind, Ali. Don't think the worst.'

She looked down at the plastic cup. But what if Gemma did have a serious illness like meningitis? Had they been foolish in not bringing her to hospital sooner?

'The fit may be linked to her fever, which in itself can be caused by a viral infection,' she heard Sam continuing. 'She has all the classic symptoms. Raised temperature, twitching and jerking and finally that brief loss of consciousness. Kids get infections all the time and recover from them.' He drank the last of the tea and tossed the cup in the bin. Leaning his elbows on his bare brown knees, he hung his head for a second, dragging his long tanned fingers through his hair.

When he raised his head, he looked so tired that Alison wanted to put her arms around him. If she was honest, as much for her own reassurance as his.

But she sat stubbornly where she was, her blonde hair falling untidily over her face. She couldn't remember the last time she had run a comb through it. She didn't care what she looked like. Or that her grey shirt and shorts were crumpled and dirty. All she wanted was for Gemma to be well. She wanted this horrible thing that had happened to them to go away and leave them in peace.

Alison didn't know how long it was they waited, but eventually the doctor emerged between the curtains and Alison felt as though her nerves were stretched to breaking point.

'Gemma has recovered from her fit,' he told them, and Sam squeezed Alison's hand. 'It was a febrile convulsion,' he went on to explain as Alison's heart refused to stop pounding.

'Probably induced by the underlying infection?' Sam queried.

The doctor nodded. 'And it appears to be nothing serious.'

Alison let out a silent sigh of relief. 'Is her temperature down?' She forced her numb mind to work.

'Yes, and as she was unconscious for only a few minutes, I think its safe to say she will make a full recovery.'

'Can we take her home?' Sam asked.

The doctor hesitated. 'The question is whether we should keep her in—maybe it would do more harm than good if we did. Many children prefer to recuperate at home rather than in a hospital environment.' He paused, glancing at Alison. 'However, as doctors you know there is always a possibility she might convulse again...'

'We'd still prefer to take her home,' Alison said without hesitation.

The doctor nodded. 'Perhaps if you sit with her in a side ward for a short while before leaving...'

Agreeing to his suggestion, Alison and Sam were taken to Gemma. A nurse was bending over her as they walked in and Alison almost gave way at the sight of Gemma's little body clad in a hospital gown.

She was sitting up, however, and looked better. But when she saw Alison and Sam, she burst into tears. Alison hurried to comfort her.

'We're here, sweetheart,' Sam said, his voice rough with emotion, his arms going round them both.

They dressed her in borrowed hospital clothes since, in her haste, Alison had brought nothing with her.

'Not long now,' Alison whispered in Gemma's ear as they sat together in the little room. But it seemed hours before they were officially discharged and Alison wasn't surprised to discover it was midday by the time they returned home.

'Someone's missed out on their beauty sleep,' Sam noted as they entered the hall and Gemma yawned.

'That makes three of us,' Alison observed as she saw the dark beard on his jaw.

Without words they ascended the stairs and Gemma made no protest as Alison changed her and laid her comfortably under a clean cotton sheet.

When her sleepy eyes closed, Alison sank down onto the futon beside Sam. A sense of peace and well-being filled her. Gemma's breathing was regular once more. Whatever had caused the infection was now gone.

'She's going to be all right,' Alison murmured sleepily, laying her head on Sam's shoulder. He turned slightly and her cheek fitted perfectly against it. She curled beside him and fell fast asleep, just as she had in those early days when they had first moved into the cottage and the future had stretched blissfully before them.

Alison woke to find herself stretched full length on the futon. The smell of coffee was wafting up from downstairs. Gemma's bed was made neatly and her toys were in a pile in the corner of the room.

Alison sat up with a start and looked at her watch. Half past five! She couldn't believe she had slept all afternoon. Hurriedly she stood up. The window was open and a soft breeze blew in. Voices, she realised, were coming from the garden.

Folding the blanket and placing it on the end of the bed, Alison went to the window. Outside on the lawn Sam was sitting in the swing seat with Gemma on his lap, a book open on the seat.

Gemma was oblivious to everything as she listened to her father. Sam's arm was around her small body, now dressed in her favourite pink dungarees. The seat swung gently to and fro and Sam laughed suddenly. Alison swallowed as she heard Gemma's gurgle.

His dark head was bent and Alison watched for some time, recalling how she had stood in this very room when they had first moved in and looked out on the garden that both she and Sam loved. It had been a wilderness then, the fruit trees untended until Sam had invested his time and interest in them.

Suddenly the memories threatened to swamp her. She pulled back, but as she did so, she caught the curtain with her shoulder. Sam's head jerked up.

'Mummy's awake,' she heard him say, and Gemma squirmed round on his lap, waving her small hands.

'Coffee's made,' Sam called, his easy smile making her heart squeeze again. A flower-filled garden, a father and daughter—a happy, indulgent picture.

'I'll shower and be down,' she called back, careful to hide the catch in her voice.

With that she left the window and went to the bathroom, undressed and showered, aware of how easy it would be to respond to Sam's presence at the cottage. How easy it would be to mend that ache inside her...and how foolish.

A thought she dwelt on as she changed into cool cotton trousers and a blue silk shirt. Before going downstairs, she sprayed on the perfume she loved best. It was Sam's favourite, a delicate but sensual scent he had chosen for her birthday.

Silly that she should wear it today! She had others to use. But somehow she couldn't stop herself. Last night she hadn't wanted him to leave—neither did she want him to leave today. She was enacting a fantasy and she knew it. But she couldn't stop herself.

And as she looked at her reflection in the mirror and saw the desire in her eyes, she didn't even try.

That evening, a sash of golden sun melted into the hills. Tea in the garden was over, and, though Gemma was still subdued, her temperature had returned to normal. She had eaten her first solid food in two days—a bowl of ice cream, a spoonful of jelly and a half a cucumber sandwich.

'I think,' said Sam as Alison collected the plates from the garden table, 'someone is ready for bed.'

Alison glanced at Gemma, who had folded herself back into Sam's arms and was lightly dozing.

'I'll bring her up, if you like—and say good-night,' he murmured as he rose and carried Gemma in his arms to the house.

Alison was to recall this remark as, after they had settled Gemma and returned downstairs, Sam paused by the front door.

'I'll be at home if you want me,' he said, and made no attempt to follow her to the kitchen.

'You're going?' she said, unable to mask her surprise.

He nodded and for a long moment they remained where they were, the silence stretching between them. Finally, unable to bring herself to ask him to stay, she dropped her gaze. The next thing she knew the door was squeaking open and he had stepped outside.

She found herself accompanying him down the garden path and at the gate he turned. The summer night was soft and mellow; his dark eyes glimmered and suddenly she noticed that he was clean-shaven. He must have shaved whilst she'd slept, she reflected, using the spare electric razor she had always kept in the bedroom.

'I think you'll have a better night,' he said as he opened the gate.

'Yes, I'll probably sleep on the futon again,' she said quickly, attempting a casual response.

'I'm at home if you want me,' he murmured. 'Though, if not, you can always ring me on my mobile. You have the number, don't you?'

She nodded, the thought occurring to her that someone might be waiting for him, somewhere other than at his flat. It was a thought that made her recall Friday night and when, without hesitation, he had come immediately to see Gemma. Had he been with someone then?

'Thank you for coming,' she said rather abruptly. 'And for looking after Gem today.'

'Would you have expected me to do otherwise?' His voice was puzzled and she shook her head.

'No, of course not. I just—'

'Alison, Gemma's welfare comes before anything. Which is why—' He stopped, catching his bottom lip between his teeth briefly before lifting his shoulders on a long sigh. 'Look, I'd better go.'

It was then she made her mistake, one that she was to spend the evening regretting. 'Do you have to?' she asked as hot colour rushed to her cheeks.

He looked at her again with a puzzled frown. 'Gemma's going to be all right,' was his reply as he closed the gate. 'So what would be the point?'

He left and Alison went back into the cottage, closing the door quickly behind her. Her face was on fire and her wounded pride felt like a stone lodged in her chest.

Why had she asked him to stay? It was inevitable that he should find someone else in time. Recalling her own words flung at him, that, estranged as they were, he was entitled to live his life as he pleased, Alison returned to reality with a bump.

He had lived apart from them for fourteen months, four of those before he left for Australia. In that time, he could have formed another relationship. And as Alison returned to the kitchen to gaze out on the dusky garden, another thought occurred to her.

Could it have been Charlotte Macdonald that day at the surgery? What if she was back in his life or, more to the point, had never left it? The assumption on Alison's part had been that their marriage had ended because of Sam's infatuation, a short-lived fling with a much younger woman.

But now she wondered if she had drawn the wrong conclusions. Had Sam's relationship with the nurse survived his ten-month stay in Australia? Was Charlotte Macdonald the reason he had returned?

Alison stiffened as suddenly her presence in Sam's life appeared as a distinct possibility.

Though Gemma seemed well the next morning, Alison decided not to go in to work. She rang Hector, who said he and Peter would see her patients between them. Sam rang her in the afternoon, made an enquiry about Gemma, then rang off quickly.

On Wednesday, Gemma was back to her normal good spirits and Alison drove in to Kennet. After surgery she spent an hour with Gemma at the park and on Thursday, just as Alison was making Gemma's tea, the phone rang.

For some reason she expected it to be Sam, but it was Lucy. 'Hi, Dr Stewart. Sorry to bother you at home, but Eila Hayward gave birth to a boy at the weekend and has asked to be fitted in tomorrow. I know Gemma wasn't well and you didn't come in on Monday...'

'I'll be in,' Alison said at once. 'Gemma's fine now. Is the appointment for the baby or Eila?'

'For the baby—mostly.' Lucy hesitated.

'Oh,' Alison remarked, aware that Lucy sounded as though she'd been about to say more.

'They live next door, remember?' Lucy said after a pause. 'Mark's a bit of a celebrity in these parts. Plays for the local soccer team.'

'Oh, yes, Eila did mention football,' Alison recalled, wondering what Lucy was getting round to.

'I like Eila,' Lucy said, again hesitantly. 'But I'm afraid I haven't much time for Mark. Poor Eila. She's...well, she's had a lot to put up with.'

Alison was surprised, since Eila had said nothing about her marriage throughout her pregnancy, not until last time when she'd commented her husband wanted a boy. And after Lucy had rung off, Alison wondered if she had wanted to say more but had thought better of it.

No doubt she would discover more tomorrow when she saw Eila.

But it wasn't of the young mother that Alison was thinking as she arrived in the car park the following morning. As usual, she prepared to meet Sam, a shiver of apprehension going through her as she saw the Mercedes in its usual spot.

By now, she told herself as she parked and locked her car, they should have struck a compromise. Each of them knew how important harmony was, if not in their private lives then in a professional sense.

Gemma was the cornerstone of their existence. Both of them accepted their roles as pivotal to Gemma's upbringing, yet neither seemed able to move in other directions.

Take Thomas Knight, the teenager with asthma, Alison pondered as she walked the towpath. After failing to locate Thomas that weekend—the weekend Gemma had been ill— she had consoled herself with the thought that had trouble arisen after Sam's imprudent counselling, Mrs Knight would have returned with Thomas.

But as it was, the sunny Friday morning seemed off to a positive start as Alison entered a calm and unflustered Reception. The small

group of patients contained none that she recognised and the desk was pleasantly clear of
queries.

'Only a couple of prescriptions to sign,'
Pam told her cheerfully as she paused. 'Dr
Trenchard and Dr Stewart are well under way.
Dr Johnson's on calls and all our computers
are up and running.'

Alison raised her eyebrows dryly. 'So, do
we have a downside?'

'Not at all. Just wait till you speak to your
first patient.'

Alison frowned curiously. 'Is it Eila
Hayward?'

'No, she's at eleven.'

'You're keeping me in suspense.' Alison
grinned.

'Well, I don't want to spoil the surprise. All
I will say is that when they made the appointment, they were chuffed to bits.'

For a moment or two, Alison hesitated, but
Pam drew her fingers across her lips in a gesture of zipped silence.

When she reached her room, Alison hurried
to search for the list usually placed on the top
of her correspondence. This morning, her desk
bore refreshingly little—a few papers bearing

red question marks and two prescriptions in need of signatures.

She was about to ring through to Reception when the phone rang. 'They're in. Are you ready?' Pam asked eagerly.

'I certainly am.' Alison smiled to herself. 'Oh, and don't forget my list, Pam. It seems to be missing.'

'Yes, well, that would have given the game away, wouldn't it?'

A few seconds later the door opened and Pam entered, the list in her hand. Behind her walked the tall, gangling figure of fourteen-year-old Thomas Knight, followed closely by his mother.

'Dr Stewart, I can't believe it, but it's true,' the older woman said as she bustled forward. 'Thomas is...well, he's not wheezing any more. Listen, he's as clear as a bell. He even did gym yesterday without once using his inhaler. I can't believe it. Can you?'

Alison looked up at Thomas. Other than the embarrassed blush on his face, illuminating a rebellious sprinkling of teenage spots, he looked wonderfully healthy.

And he wasn't wheezing.

A fact that Thomas himself was soon to confirm.

CHAPTER SIX

IT WAS several minutes before Mrs Knight sat down and Thomas was able to relate what had happened. 'I had a gym session yesterday,' he told Alison, 'and usually I take my puffer as soon as I start getting wheezy. But that never happened.'

'You mean you didn't wheeze at all?' Alison asked.

'I do Dr Stewart's exercises every day. I haven't had a bad attack since I saw him.'

Alison glanced at Mrs Knight who was nodding firmly. 'That's right. He started them as soon as he left here last time and did them each day and—'

'So you think these exercises have helped, Thomas?' Alison cut in quickly.

'Yes. I don't think I'll need the inhaler again.'

At this, Alison shook her head. 'Thomas, I know you may be confident about these exercises working—but for safety's sake, you must always have your inhaler with you.'

'Dr Stewart said that,' Thomas replied immediately. 'But I can control an attack now if it comes on, like this.' Thomas pinched his nose with his thumb and index finger and looked at his watch. After a while he let go and took a few shallow breaths, slowly returning to normal breathing.

'Why did you look at your watch?' Alison asked curiously.

'I can get up to fifty seconds now, holding my breath.'

'And that's the technique?'

'Some of it,' responded the youngster enthusiastically. 'Dr Stewart explained that, as an asthmatic, I was hyperventilating when I got an attack. I thought it was the other way round, but it's not. Anyway, what he taught me in the first session really worked and I just kept it up.'

'I see,' Alison replied cautiously, 'but all the same, Thomas, please, never go out without your inhaler.'

'I make certain he takes it with him,' Mrs Knight interrupted, sitting forward on her seat. 'You know, I thought the whole thing was ludicrous at first. Then when I saw Thomas doing these exercises three times a day regularly, I was shocked. I mean, Thomas isn't one to stick at anything for very long, let alone boring exercises.'

'They're not boring, Mum,' Thomas said quietly. 'They help me.'

'I know, dear,' his mother replied patiently, 'but Dr Stewart said you need to do a proper course with him. Which is why we're here this morning.' She glanced at Alison. 'Thomas had a free period, so I thought I'd just get you to check him. Better safe than sorry, I always say.'

'I'm all right, Mum. I don't need examining,' Thomas protested, clearly embarrassed at being interrogated in such a fashion.

Alison found herself in a quandary. She had been highly sceptical of Sam's approach with this boy. But Thomas appeared to be confident the technique was working. She didn't want to discourage him. To give Thomas credit, he had persisted with the exercises since seeing Sam and his health seemed better.

On the other hand, she was still annoyed with Sam for instigating this dilemma. What should she do now? She herself had no idea of how the technique worked or whether this whole scenario happened to be a lucky coincidence, a thought obviously shared by Mrs Knight who had brought Thomas along today.

Finally, in order to save the youngster further embarrassment yet reassure his mother, she suggested Thomas return the following week, intending to sort out the muddle with Sam meanwhile.

'Oh, he's got an appointment booked already,' Mrs Knight assured Alison as they stood up. 'I want him to come to that special asthma clinic he was telling me about.'

When the tall young man and his mother had left, Alison gritted her teeth. Sam's presumption that he could start up such a new and obviously revolutionary asthma clinic on the practice premises, without having brought it to Hector's notice, let alone hers, was beyond words.

She scribbled a reminder on her pad to speak to Hector, though the fact remained, she reluctantly accepted, that when she did, it would be a case of the evidence weighing against her. Her less than effective management of Thomas's asthma versus the wonder cure provided by Sam!

Later that morning Eila Hayward appeared, her baby in her arms. Anthony was asleep and required only a swift inspection of his nappy rash to resolve Eila's infant worries. He seemed a contented seven-pounder with a cloud of black hair and a healthy complexion.

However, as the consultation wore on, Alison's suspicions grew that all was not as it should be. Attempting to ignore the information given her by Lucy, Alison asked Eila if she was feeling well.

'Yes, fine,' Eila said with a smile that didn't convince Alison.

'Are you eating and getting enough rest?'

'Yes, Anthony's a good baby. He goes through until about five.'

'And you go back to bed afterwards?'

Eila's eyes lowered. 'Well, sometimes. But I like to get up and clean the house.'

'Would you sleep on if you could?' Alison persisted.

It was a moment or two before Eila shook her head. 'No, I'm awake before Anthony sometimes. I do find it a little difficult to switch off.'

Alison was concerned at the dark rings under Eila's eyes and her noticeable pallor. She had lost a great deal of weight since the baby's birth and, unlike her old self, seemed to take little interest in her clothes or hair.

'We're running a mother and baby clinic on Monday afternoons,' Alison suggested easily.

'Why don't you bring Anthony along?' Without Eila taking her into her confidence, there was little she could do, and the clinic suggestion was her only alternative.

'I'll think about it,' Eila said quickly, standing up and gathering Anthony in her arms.

It was an abrupt exit and Alison sat quietly for a few moments, wondering what was worrying the young woman. Something sparked in Alison's mind. Was it a remark Eila had made—or perhaps something Lucy had said?

Before she was able to decide, there was a knock on the open door and Alison looked up to see Sam standing there.

'Sam, I saw Thomas and his mother,' she blurted, attempting to ignore the dragging clutch at her ribs that always accompanied her first sight of him.

'Did you?' he murmured vaguely, and he walked towards her.

'He's had some success with your breathing technique—'

'Good,' he interrupted distantly, glancing at his watch. 'Look, Alison, I'd like to stop, but I have to hurry. I've several visits to make before lunch. I wanted to speak to you before I left—about Hector's invitation. I wanted you to know I had nothing—absolutely nothing to do with it.'

Alison frowned, taken aback. 'What invitation?'

'You mean he hasn't…?' Sam gave a little groan and thrust his hands into his pockets. 'Well, prepare yourself. No doubt he'll approach you today.'

'Prepare for what?' she asked with a shrug.

'Just be warned, that's all. A simple no might well be the best answer from both of us.'

Alison rose to her feet and walked round her desk. 'Sam, I'm afraid I don't understand.'

'Hector is getting engaged. Didn't you know?'

Alison almost laughed. 'But he's been a bachelor for years!'

'Yes, and I suppose we assumed he would remain one,' Sam replied, one eyebrow jerking up.

'When did you find out?'

'On Wednesday, but you weren't here then, were you?'

Alison shook her head. 'I'm at Kennet on Wednesdays. And Thursday was my day off. Though I suppose he could have rung me on my mobile…'

'No, I think he would have waited for to-day,' Sam murmured. 'Probably wanted to tell you in person.'

'Yes, perhaps he does,' Alison agreed, sensing something in Sam's tone that she didn't recognise. 'I'm surprised—but delighted,' she added quickly. 'However, I can't see what it has to do with us.'

'Quite a bit,' Sam responded darkly. 'He's planned something of a celebration. He wants us to meet her. And he's asked... Well, he's asked us as his guests—and Peter and his girl-friend.'

Alison tried to digest this information, whilst at the same time wondering what else Sam was hiding. 'You mean just the six of us?'

Sam nodded. 'Look, can we discuss this later?'

'Sam, what aren't you telling me?' she persisted following him to the door.

But as he stepped out into the hall, her next patient was walking towards them and Sam moved aside. 'I'll ring you—OK?'

Alison watched him move away, wondering what it was that he found so difficult to tell her. Surely a meeting with Hector's prospective fiancée was nothing to be so alarmed about? However, she was concerned that

Hector hadn't told her what he was planning. Having no idea who his girlfriend was—or even why Hector was insisting they meet—it all seemed rather clandestine.

Something, too, in the way Sam hadn't quite met her eyes made her feel uneasy. But whatever it was, Sam's words—'A simple no might be the best answer from both of us'—indicated his disapproval of Hector's news. Perhaps Sam had been concerned it might turn into one of those embarrassing occasions, fielding questions about their own relationship?

It was at the end of her surgery that Hector met her in Reception. He looked somewhat askance as he handed a pile of records back to Lucy and then turned toward Alison.

'Have you seen Sam?' he asked, which brought a smile to her lips since Sam had asked her the same question about Hector.

'Yes, but only for a minute. He was leaving for his calls.'

Hector nodded slowly, as though debating within himself his next question. 'Are you finished now?'

'Yes…why?'

'Have lunch with me, Ali, would you?'

It was then that Alison knew there was something wrong. She couldn't bring herself to refuse, both her curiosity and alarm mounting, and ten minutes later she found herself sitting opposite Hector in the small Lamstone bistro, fifty yards along the waterfront, which Hector used as his bolt-hole.

'I'm sure word's got round to you by now that I'm engaged,' Hector divulged after she'd ordered a simple omelette in preference to Hector's suggestion of dish of the day. 'Well, my finacée Annabelle has asked us all as house guests for a weekend...'

Alison, with her mouth falling open, was already shaking her head, but Hector continued relentlessly.

'The poor girl is clueless,' Hector sighed, his frown pleating under his shock of grey hair, 'of what a doctor's life involves, and...' Hector paused, his eyes revolving helplessly around the room. 'And before we settle on a date, she would dearly love to meet you all. I've absolutely no hope of getting her to say yes until she does. Alison, I can't tell you what this means to me.'

A remark that Alison totally identified with as she sat wordlessly in front of her half-finished omelette.

*　　*　　*

The telephone rang at half past seven that evening. Even before Alison picked it up she knew it was Sam. She was still trying to come to terms with what had happened at lunchtime and her reaction to it, which she had yet to explain to Sam.

'Did Hector speak to you?' Sam asked at once.

'Yes. Why didn't you tell me what he had in mind, Sam?'

'Because I knew it would upset you.' He paused for some time. 'I did try, if you remember, but we don't seem to operate on the same wavelength these days.'

'No, we don't. And Hector hasn't helped. He asked me to lunch and landed his bombshell then.'

She heard Sam's soft chuckle. 'I didn't even get lunch.'

'No, well, I suspect I was a harder nut to crack.'

'So you said no, then?'

She paused. 'Not quite,' she admitted reluctantly.

'Is Gem still up?' Sam asked as she was about to suggest he come over and talk the problem through.

'I was just about to read her a story.'

'Would it be all right if I came over and said goodnight?'

'I think you'd better,' Alison sighed. 'And afterwards perhaps we can decide on what we're going to do.'

Alison hurried from the bedroom where she had just taken Sam's call, checked that Gemma was playing with her toys in the nursery and then changed. She chose a sleeveless, pale blue sundress which she had bought the previous year.

It was made of a soft, silky material that showed off her long bare legs and slender hips. Clare had raised an eyebrow when she'd seen it and after that Alison had been reluctant to wear it out. But it was more comfortable than anything else in her wardrobe and certainly perfect for the humid evening.

Sam arrived, as he had on the night of Gemma's illness, not more than fifteen minutes later. Alison had just finished brushing her hair up into a clip when the door squeaked open and Sam's voice echoed through the house.

'Dadda!' Gemma screamed delightedly, and Alison swept her up in her arms as she ran from the nursery.

'We're upstairs,' Alison called down, and Sam appeared, dressed in faded denim shorts and a colourful shirt that looked more suitable for a tropical island than an English village.

He straddled the gate and held out his arms. 'Hello, sweetheart.' He chuckled, taking Gemma and giving her a hug. 'How's my girl?'

Gemma held her father's rapt attention as they went into the nursery and began to play with toys on the floor.

Alison sat on the bed and watched. Suddenly Sam glanced up and the smile disappeared from his face. 'Have I interrupted something by any chance?' he muttered, scowling.

'What do you mean?' she asked, aware that he seemed to be scrutinising her.

'Just that you're dressed to go out, aren't you?'

'No...' She hesitated, feeling self-conscious. 'As a matter of fact, if you hadn't rung, I would have rung you.'

'Would you?' His dark eyes flashed for a moment—until her next remark.

'Of course. I wanted to get things sorted out before we drifted into an arrangement that neither of us wanted.'

'Oh,' he said, turning back to Gemma.

'And there's Thomas Knight,' she added quickly.

'Yes…OK,' he murmured, his attention now totally absorbed by Gemma and the clockwork pig she insisted her father wind up.

Alison said no more and decided to give them some time alone. Busying herself with other chores, it wasn't until she heard Sam's deep and level tone and noticed the absence of Gemma's chatter that she guessed he was reading her a story.

Finally there was silence. Alison found herself standing in the middle of her bedroom, listening, her gaze going to her reflection in the long mirror. Did she really look as though she had been going out tonight? Had she seen a flicker of interest in Sam's eyes as he'd gazed at her?

It was a pretty dress, she had to admit. The pale blue was the same shade as her eyes and the slightly shorter hem flattered her long legs. Her self-confidence had taken a knock in the wake of Sam's affair. Charlotte Macdonald had not only been attractive, but bright and intelligent—and, of course, young.

Not that thirty-three was old, she told herself as she stared in the mirror at the lithe figure in the sundress. Not old, but not as fresh and inviting as twenty-five—obviously.

Alison closed her eyes, shutting out the feelings of jealousy. She wasn't going to allow them to spoil tonight. She mustn't. All too swiftly their meetings lately had turned into confrontations. They were both adults—separated adults. They should be able to handle their differences by now.

In the nursery, Sam had switched on the pink light and was sitting on Gemma's bed, stroking her soft blonde curls. He seemed far away, content to lavish his attention on his sleeping daughter.

Alison lingered, watching them, resting against the door, sharing the silence that seemed too peaceful to break. Gemma's fair eyelashes lay on her rosy cheeks like lace, her breathing soft and regular.

'I'll be downstairs,' Alison whispered eventually, but it wasn't until some while later that Sam joined her in the garden. She was sitting on the swing seat and he sank down on it, too, the heaviness of his body indenting the cushions beside her. His arm brushed hers briefly and she inhaled the musky, familiar scent, sucking in an involuntary breath.

When she glanced at him, his mouth was grim, but soft, as though half of him was still upstairs with Gemma. His dark brown eyes held no hint of what he was thinking, but she could guess. And she felt sad for them both, that on a perfect summer's evening they seemed so distanced.

Once upon a time they would have sat here and his arm would have slid round her, bringing her against him, his lips meeting hers in a warm and passionate kiss. She would have snuggled against him, drawn her bare feet up onto the seat, luxuriated in his presence.

'She's a beautiful child,' he whispered almost to himself, echoing Alison's earlier thoughts. 'She's like you, Ali. All those lovely blonde curls and that gorgeous complexion...'

He reached out, lifted a lock of hair from her neck and tucked it gently behind her ear. The gesture was natural, so familiar that she didn't stir, her body waiting—as it had always waited—for his next movement.

She remembered their love-making so vividly. Once he would have taken her face between his hands, drawn his fingers up into her hair with infinite slowness, and she would have moaned softly, unable to wait for their passage over her skin. Even now she could feel her hair falling down at the sweep of his fingers, making space for his lips as he leaned forward to kiss her neck.

Unbidden, her eyes travelled downward to the tanned hollow at his throat. His shirt lay open and his skin gleamed in the dying sunshine. He was such a virile male, so well made, so sexy. Bone so sleekly hewn beneath grainy dark skin and that sensual aura shining around him into which she melted with such ease and hunger.

He drew his hand away, leaving a desolate emptiness. She looked down at her clenched hands. She didn't want to feel like this, so vulnerable, as though he had reached inside her and touched her heart. She made an effort to gather herself and sat upright on the seat, effectively putting distance between them.

'I suppose we had better get the subject of Hector over, hadn't we?' he asked shortly.

'Yes,' she replied, lifting her head. 'Sam, I have no desire to spend a weekend away—anywhere—without Gemma. Especially since she hasn't been well.'

'My sentiments exactly.'

Her head spun round. 'I mean,' she fumbled, 'I don't suppose it will be the last time we'll be asked—'

'So we'll start as we mean to go on,' he interrupted firmly. 'That's fine by me.'

'Yes,' she agreed, somewhat at a loss for words now. She hadn't expected his compliance. 'An evening dinner, yes, but two days...'

'Quite out of the question.'

Alison looked at him. She could tell nothing by his expression. 'What did Peter think?' she asked cautiously.

'Oh, Peter's all for it.' He shrugged indifferently. 'But Peter would be. After all, he's not married.'

'And neither are we,' she reminded him. 'We're separated.'

He nodded, apparently in agreement. 'Which brings us back to square one. What do we tell Hector?'

'The truth,' Alison answered crisply.

'Is that what you told him at lunch today—the truth?'

She flushed, recalling her reluctance to give Hector an answer. 'I was caught by surprise—' she began.

'As I was.' Sam cut her short. 'However, if you remember, I did give you a head start.'

'Well, yes. But I still had a shock when Hector made it plain he wasn't going to propose until after his fiancée met us. In a sense, making it our responsibility to help him.'

'Which is ridiculous,' Sam commented.

'But, of course, you didn't tell him it was?' Alison sneaked a glance and was satisfied to see that he, too, had no answer.

'The point is,' he sighed after a long pause, 'Hector is so damned convincing—he makes you feel obliged to put in an appearance.'

'Well, why don't you go?' Alison suggested.

'On my own? What, and play gooseberry to *two* couples?' He laughed shortly. 'Alison, you've got to be joking.'

'Well, we'd only play gooseberry anyway, wouldn't we? If we both went?'

A smile crossed his lips. 'Yes, but it could be interesting. Hector in wooing mode…?'

Alison smiled. 'I'm amazed none of us guessed.'

'The sly old dog.'

'I wonder what she's like…'

Suddenly they looked at each other and Alison began to laugh. 'I don't know what we find so funny,' she murmured. 'We should be annoyed with Hector for putting us in this position.'

'And finding himself a fiancée so late in life. Why couldn't he have done it when we were together? I've always wanted to stay at a country seat.'

Alison turned slowly to stare at him. 'A country seat?'

Sam nodded. 'You know who his fiancée is, don't you?'

'I've no idea,' Alison said in alarm. 'I was so busy trying to think of an excuse not to go, I didn't ask.'

Sam's eyebrows shot up. 'She's Annabelle Reid.'

It was a moment before the name registered and Alison's jaw dropped as she gasped. 'You mean, *the* Annabelle Reid, divorced wife of Theo Reid?'

Sam nodded slowly. 'The very same.'

Alison rested her head back on the cushion, hiding her amusement. Hector certainly was a dark horse. No wonder there had been so much secrecy. The papers had had a feeding frenzy over the break-up of the wealthy businessman's third marriage.

Sam's voice suddenly broke into her thoughts. 'Why? If you'd known who it was, would it make any difference to your answer?'

It was then that Alison found herself smiling again as she looked at Sam and wondered what he would say if she replied yes. But just at that moment the phone rang and she was saved from the temptation of doing so.

It was Clare, for their usual Friday night gossip. But when she knew that Sam was visiting, she said she would call again tomorrow. On Alison's return to the garden, Sam was standing up, gazing out through the fruit trees, his hand thrust into the pockets of his shorts, one shoulder propped against the timber shed.

'That was Clare,' she told him, and he turned, leaning his back against the shed.

'Did she mention that I gave Robbie a hand yesterday evening with some of the greenhouses?'

'No.' Alison frowned. It was unusual for Clare not to have said anything.

'It was nothing much. The cost of new glass was pretty steep, so I offered to help replace some of the framework with Robbie. My DIY skills aren't that great but we managed between us.'

'Did you see Robbie after his accident, then?'

'Yes, I called in to see if I could help and one thing led to another.'

'I see.'

'You don't mind, do you?'

'Mind what?'

'Me seeing Robbie.' His dark eyes were watching her under their hooded lids and she shrugged.

'No, why should I? Robbie and Clare could do with the help.'

'Yes, that was why I offered. I know it hasn't been easy for them. To be honest, I simply don't know how your mother coped after your father left.' He stopped and, folding his arms across his chest, gazed down at his feet.

'It was a struggle,' Alison said as she had the sudden and painful picture of her mother managing the market garden after her father had gone. She'd been fourteen when he'd left home to live with another woman and Clare had been eleven. Without the help of Robbie's parents, who were family friends, Alison knew the business and their livelihood would have gone under.

'I admire Robbie and Clare for taking the nursery on as they did,' Sam remarked quietly. 'Even though they were childhood sweethearts, it's been tough going.'

Alison nodded. 'And they are still as much in love as ever.'

Clare had never wanted babies, whilst Alison had. As the years had passed, they'd seemed to have the marriages and husbands they'd dreamed of. So unlike their mother, who had never really recovered from her loss. Alison always believed the stroke that had killed her had been as the result of shock. Not that her father's second marriage had endured. He had separated from his second wife just before his death in a car accident.

'So, what are we going to do?' Sam asked, his deep voice bringing Alison sharply back from the past.

'About Hector?' She shrugged. 'What can we do but tell him the truth?'

'Yes, but *what* truth?'

'That we feel it's inappropriate to accept the invitation. Perhaps we could organise a dinner or something more…er…suitable?'

Sam slowly raised himself. 'OK. We'll speak to him on Monday before surgery.'

She nodded as they walked into the kitchen. 'Would you like a coffee?' she heard herself asking, though she sensed—again—that he wouldn't accept.

'Thanks, but I'd better get on.'

The last of the sunlight was streaming through the kitchen and filled the room with golden rays. Bathed in the glow, dressed in his colourful shirt and shorts, he looked almost as though he had just walked off some tropical beach. His dark skin reflected the sand and sea and holidays past, a reminder of times shared, of beaches explored on deserted islands and scented evenings, walking barefoot and care-free.

She shivered. He stared at her with those deep brown eyes that made her suck in air—air that scored her throat and entered her lungs with a whoosh. Nothing had changed in all the years she had known him. He was a habit hard to kick.

'Kiss Gem for me,' he said as he suddenly moved, and she started, realising that he was leaving and that her thoughts had been half in the present and half in the past. Dragging them back quickly, she accompanied him to the front door.

'See you Monday.' His eyes found hers for a brief moment, then his long legs carried him swiftly up the path and through the gate. The soft growl of the car engine faded into the night.

Then silence…

Alison closed the door, let out the air trapped in her chest and walked into the garden. The thought struck her, as she sank down onto the swing seat, that once again they had forgotten to speak about Thomas.

She sighed, putting the thought out of mind until Monday.

Her hand felt its way to the cushions beside her. She left it there, reluctant to move it away.

CHAPTER SEVEN

HAVING worried all weekend about speaking to Hector on Monday, Alison arrived at the surgery to find that Hector was off sick.

'Flu,' said Lucy as she brought in the morning's list of patients, heavily peppered with Hector's patients. 'Sorry, but Dr Johnson's on calls and Dr Stewart has the other half of Dr Trenchard's list.'

'I'm sorry to hear Hector's ill,' Alison murmured, sorry in more ways than one since the subject of the weekend would now have to wait. 'Well, we'd better get started, then, Lucy—and have you a coffee going? I think I'm probably going to need it this morning.'

'I'll bring you one in.' Lucy grinned. 'Triple strength.'

Fortunately, Alison's morning ran smoothly, despite the overspill of Hector's patients. There were the usual assortment of minor illnesses, repeat prescriptions and a few summer visitors who were classed as temporary residents. But during the afternoon a rush of emergencies materi-alised. A young man with an

134

inflamed appendix, whom Alison admitted to hospital, a farmer who had wounded his hand beyond surgery repair and a fourteen-year-old with a very high temperature.

Victoria Reid had spent the weekend with a raised temperature and swollen glands. Alison saw her immediately and was glad she'd done so. The lymph nodes in her neck, armpits and groin were swollen, accompanied by a raging sore throat. The discovery of an enlarged spleen as Alison examined her abdomen confirmed her diagnosis of glandular fever.

'Can't she have an antibiotic?' the mother demanded, as Alison ordered blood tests.

'Not with glandular fever,' Alison was careful to explain. 'The treatment is rest, to allow the body's immune system to destroy the virus.'

'But wouldn't an antibiotic do that quicker? My niece had a gland problem and she had a five-day course and she was better in no time.'

'I don't know what was wrong with your niece,' Alison returned swiftly, 'but when ampicillin is given in the mistaken belief that glandular fever is a bacterial infection, it does far more harm than good. Let's confirm the glandular fever and we'll go from there. But for now the answer is, as I say, complete rest.'

'How long for?' Mrs Reid demanded.

'A month to six weeks, possibly longer.'

'But that's out of the question—we're going abroad for the summer.'

'I don't think—' Alison began but was stopped in mid-sentence by the woman's angry interruption.

'There must be a mistake here,' Mrs Reid spluttered. 'Victoria has swollen glands, yes, and is a bit off colour, but glandular fever—well, I've never heard of such a thing. I'm sure you must be wrong. We usually see Dr Trenchard but was told he was ill.' She stood up, taking hold of her daughter's wrist. 'I insist we be seen by someone else—a permanent member of staff.'

Alison stood up slowly, shocked and angry. The inference that her diagnosis was less accurate because she worked part time at the surgery was rude and offensive. However, since Victoria seemed distressed and any further argument would, no doubt, increase her anxiety, Alison asked Lucy to show the Reids into a treatment room.

'What an unpleasant woman,' Lucy remarked a few minutes later as she put her head round the door.

Making no comment, but explaining what had happened, Alison suggested that either Sam or Peter, when he returned, be made aware of the situation before seeing Victoria.

Alison braved her way through the rest of the afternoon, but there was no doubt the remark had unnerved her. And when, at the end of surgery, Sam appeared at her door, Alison was eager to know what had transpired.

'It's glandular fever all right,' Sam told her as he sat down in a chair, a mug of coffee in his hand. 'I haven't any doubt of that. However, the mother didn't like it much. I don't think she'll fully go along with the diagnosis until we get the blood-test results through.'

'I don't know why she reacted so badly.' Alison frowned as she, too, sipped at the coffee Lucy had just made her. 'She certainly needn't have been so rude.'

'I suspect she feels Victoria's illness reflects on her behaviour,' Sam remarked cryptically.

'Really, but how?' Alison asked with another frown.

'She was talking to her daughter when I went in—or rather, they were arguing about a boyfriend who Mrs Reid disapproves of.'

Alison nodded in sudden understanding. 'You mean the link between teenagers kissing and passing the virus?'

Sam quirked an eyebrow. 'A rather fraught situation, I'm afraid. The parents divorced two years ago. Mrs Reid pointed out that since then there have been difficulties at school.'

Alison sighed. 'Well, Victoria is almost fifteen. She is likely to have a boyfriend.'

'Obviously this particular one doesn't meet Mum's criteria.'

'What about the father?' Alison asked curiously.

'He's remarried and started a new family. It was Victoria's school who discovered her truanting.'

'To be with the boy?'

'Apparently so. Hence the holiday abroad.'

Alison now felt rather sorry for Mrs Reid. 'And if the tests are positive, they'll have to abandon the idea altogether?'

'The joys of parenting,' Sam murmured dryly. 'I suppose none of us know how we will cope in such a situation—but, heck, fourteen is desperately young to be in a relationship.'

'Not so much these days,' Alison answered reflectively. 'And who knows what will be acceptable by the time Gemma is fourteen?'

'I don't care what the fashion is then or now,' Sam said firmly. 'A fourteen-year-old daughter of mine will—' He stopped abruptly as Alison's eyebrows rose slowly.

They were silent then and Alison knew they were both thinking of the future and what it might hold. Would Sam's interpretation of parenting be different to hers? If they had stayed together, perhaps not.

Sam suddenly rose to his feet and, drawing his hand over his jaw, pushed the chair to one side. 'Anyway, it's time I went. A pity Hector wasn't in today.'

'Yes.' She stood up. 'But at least we've made a decision.'

'Spending a weekend away together would be out of the question.'

She nodded firmly. 'Of course.'

Outside they could hear the girls in Reception preparing to leave. Sam said rather hurriedly as he reached the door. 'By the way, Thomas is coming in after school on Friday. Would you like to sit in?'

'Perhaps I should wait until your new clinic starts?' she said challengingly.

'New clinic?' He tilted his dark head, his eyes narrowing as he stared at her. 'I'm sorry, I'm not with you.'

'Mrs Knight said you had one in mind...'

'Did she now?' His frown slowly cleared. 'I happened to mention I ran clinics in Australia and it was her suggestion that I should set one up here. I replied that I could only do so with Hector's approval, and indeed, with agreement from all members of staff.' His mouth curved up in a smile. 'Anyway, the offer's open for Friday if you're interested.'

After he left, Alison sat for a while, attempting to recall what Mrs Knight had specifically said about an asthma clinic, but it was only as she drove home that she realised she had no reason to disbelieve Sam.

Why, then, had she been so swift to accept Mrs Knight's version?

On Friday afternoon, Alison found Mrs Knight and Thomas in Reception.

'How are you, Thomas?' Alison asked as the young man stood up.

'Great, thanks, Dr Stewart.'

'I'm pleased to hear it.' Alison turned to his mother. 'We have no plans to set up a special asthma clinic as yet, Mrs Knight, but I'm very pleased this technique appears to have helped Thomas.'

'Yes, well, I must have been mistaken about the clinic.' Mrs Knight shrugged, pushing her son into the hall. 'But if it's helped Thomas I'm sure it will help a lot of other people.'

A fact that Alison couldn't argue with since Thomas appeared to be in the peak of health. As she accompanied the Knights into Sam's room, she asked if Mrs Knight would object to her presence, a request which neither of the Knights opposed.

Sam smiled and with a look that indicated he was pleased she had joined them he began his examination of Thomas's chest and pulse.

Alison seated herself at the back of the room, whilst Sam answered Thomas's many questions. 'The shallow breathing technique will reduce your overbreathing,' Sam assured him. 'With this method you'll increase your natural production of steroids. In time there will be no need for you to inhale artificial ones.'

'I always thought deep breathing was good for you,' Mrs Knight said whilst her son practised the method.

'Asthmatics overbreathe,' Sam explained once more. 'This results in a deficit of carbon dioxide which in turn reduces the level of oxygen in blood and tissues.'

'Will I have to do the breathing all my life?' Thomas asked.

'As a preventative, you'll whittle the technique down to a few minutes a day. Like the food you eat and the exercise you take, practising it will become automatic.'

Alison watched Thomas pinch his nose and hold his breath. He timed himself and after a while released his fingers. 'I'm up to sixty seconds,' he said, clearly pleased with himself.

'Good.' Sam nodded. 'And remember the control pause, as it's called, is the measure of your health. The longer it is, the healthier you are.'

'I could only do fifteen seconds of holding my breath at first,' Thomas replied. 'So I must be really healthy now.'

'Just remember to carry your inhaler with you,' Sam warned. 'It's early days yet.'

'That's what I tell him, Dr Stewart,' Mrs Knight said. 'You know, I tried the breathing—like you said I should—when I had my panic attack, and it worked.'

Sam hid a smile as he glanced at Alison. 'I'm glad to hear it.'

'So when does Thomas have to see you again?' Mrs Knight asked quickly as she stood up.

'Make an appointment for next week and we'll see how he's shaping up.'

Mrs Knight threw a cursory frown at Alison as she left. But Sam was smiling broadly as he closed the door. 'Well, what do you think?' he asked her.

'Of Thomas?' She nodded. 'He seems to be better. Does every asthmatic respond in the same way?'

'Children and teenagers are especially swift at learning the technique,' Sam replied. 'But I prefer to see patients for four or five days consecutively. The method needs to be explained and practised.'

'But it does seem to work.'

Sam nodded. 'I was astonished at the results of clinical trials in Australia. The majority of patients responded, young and old alike.'

'And you'd like to pursue the technique here?'

'I think it deserves a chance,' Sam replied somewhat evasively.

Alison rose and, going to the window, looked out over the river. She crossed her arms and leaned her head on the window-frame, deep in thought. 'Well, I'm certain Hector will see your point of view.'

Sam came to stand behind her. 'I'm more concerned that you do.'

She sensed him there and suppressed a shiver. 'Why is it so important to you that I should?'

'Because I've always had your support in the past,' he said quietly, and she felt him so close, so near that her skin prickled. Before she could move, his hands clasped her shoulders and he turned her slowly round until, facing him, she could do nothing but look into his eyes.

'Once, Ali,' he murmured, 'we managed to talk about anything and sort it out. Absolutely anything. I don't understand. Where did it all go wrong?'

She had asked herself that question a thousand times and had never found an answer. What had made him seek the comfort of another woman's arms? Had their love not been strong enough?

It was a question she had never been able to ask him either. Something had always held her back. Pride perhaps. Or rejection. Hearing words that would cut to the quick. She had never demanded an answer to infidelity, as some wives would have. But, then, she had been living in her own private hell. Fighting a depression so deep and despairing after Gemma's birth that she'd been unable to function, either physically or mentally.

'For God's sake, Ali,' Sam whispered hoarsely as his hands tightened on her shoulders, 'what went wrong? I know I moved out of the cottage, but—'

'You moved out, Sam, because you couldn't bear to stay with me.'

'That's not true.' He shook her a little as if to reinforce his point. 'I left because you wanted me to. You had no room for me in that sealed-off world of yours. You wouldn't listen to reason—you cut me off. And there was nothing I could do to reach you.'

Alison shook herself free, his hands falling away as though they had been burnt. 'what did you expect, Sam. *Forgiveness?*

He looked at her for a long while, as if regarding a stranger. Then he said slowly, 'If that's what it took to get us back together again—then yes. We all make mistakes. That doesn't mean a marriage has to end. We could have worked at it—'

'Sam, we've said all there is to say,' she cut in icily. She walked to the door, her body trembling. She didn't want him to see her like this. She didn't want him to know how vulnerable she still was.

'How many times have you walked away, Ali?' he demanded in a voice so low she could barely hear him. 'Are you going to walk away again? OK, I can accept your disapproval on a professional level—I had no right to think I automatically had your support. That was wrong of me. But on a personal level, we have Gemma and each other to consider, our lives before us... Ali, you have to face this—'

The phone rang and Alison stared at it, her heart hammering. She felt too numb to think or speak and she stood there for a moment until she managed to take a breath and swallow. 'You'd better answer it,' she managed, her voice breaking as she stared at him. As he went to silence it, she fled.

Hector hadn't returned to work that week so Alison was surprised to see his car arrive outside the cottage on Sunday. It was midday and she had just put Gemma down for a nap. From the window she saw Hector's racing green car glide gracefully to a halt.

Wearing shorts and T-shirt, Alison opened the front door to welcome him. A breeze swept in around her long, tanned legs. Hector, dressed in a polo shirt and flawlessly white trousers, paused on the doorstep.

'What a lovely surprise. Are you well?' Alison asked as he bent forward to kiss her cheek.

'Never better.' Hector grinned. 'It was just a summer cold I think.'

'Come in, Alison invited. 'Clare's with me. She'll be pleased to see you.'

'No, I won't disturb you.' He handed her a buff-coloured envelope on which was written her name.

Alison frowned. 'What's this, Hector?'

'I'm just the messenger,' he told her mysteriously. 'Annie's been agonising over the dilemma, poor girl. I'm afraid, once again, it was my fault. I should have discussed the situation with her.'

'Hector, I'm afraid I don't understand—'

'Just read and digest, my sweet. Forgive an old man for being such a duffer. My love to Clare and Gem.'

'Hector, wait—'

But the white-clad figure was already striding down the garden path, turning to wave at the gate. 'See you tomorrow,' he called cheerfully.

When Alison returned to the garden, Clare looked up curiously. A floppy sunhat fell over her eyes and she glanced at the envelope in Alison's hand.

Alison picked up her sunshades, sat on one of the steamer chairs and opened it. 'I wonder what Hector's up to,' she mused with a puzzled smile.

'Nice notepaper.' Clare grinned, edging forward to look at the letter.

'It's from Annabelle Reid,' Alison said in surprise.

'Hector's fiancée?'

Alison nodded, her heart racing as she read out the single paragraph. 'She apologises for placing Sam and me in an embarrassing position—Hector hadn't made it clear we were living apart. And she asks...if we would like to join them at Glencourt—with Gemma—for August bank holiday.' Alison looked up at Clare and added with amusement, 'Separate suites will be prepared for our stay.'

'Ali, that's fantastic,' Clare said breathlessly. 'Glencourt? Wasn't that the country mansion in all the newspapers last year?'

'Yes, probably,' Alison murmured vaguely.

'You will go now, won't you?' Clare asked.

'I don't know.' Alison shrugged. 'This all seems rather a coincidence. I have a feeling Hector knew we were going to refuse.'

'What if he did?' Clare pouted as she handed the letter back to Alison. 'He wants your support, that's all. And Gem will have you and Sam all to herself for two whole days.'

'That's what I'm worried about,' Alison replied doubtfully. 'I don't want to be alone with Sam for that amount of time.'

'But you won't be,' Clare pointed out with a shrug. 'There will be other people there. You told me Peter and his girlfriend had been invited, didn't you?'

'Yes. Do you think there will be others?'

'Bound to be. Oh, Ali, how exciting.'

Alison nodded slowly. 'Well, perhaps this does change things a bit. We were going to take Gem to the wildlife park just before she was ill, but never did. It would be nice for Gem.'

'Well, there you are, then,' Clare said delightedly.

Alison looked at her sister under the brim of her straw hat. 'Clare, I'm trying to be sensible—don't you see? It will be a gorgeous place, a fantastic setting and yet with the way things have been between Sam and I—'

'Which is all the more reason to get back on track,' Clare observed as she sank against the lounger. 'Ali, give yourself permission to *enjoy*, OK, so it's a dream weekend. You won the lottery. Or you got first prize in a draw. Just think of it as that. You may never have the chance again.'

Alison leaned her elbows on her bare knees and studied the faded thongs of her flip-flops. She'd have to buy new clothes, of course— and something for Gem… What was the dress code for something like this?

'I'll come shopping with you,' Clare said, reading her thoughts. 'You'll be too mean with yourself to splash out.'

'I haven't decided to go yet,' mumbled Alison darkly, and drew a groan of exasperation from Clare.

'You'll be sorry if you don't,' Clare said with impossible logic.

And Alison had the sneaking suspicion that, as always, Clare was right.

On Monday, the temperature soared. When she left Gemma with Clare the garden centre was already busy, the fine weather encouraging people to browse. At work, the windows were thrown open and the door to Sam's room opened as Alison was about to ascend the staircase.

'Ali?' Sam called, and she paused, noting a beige-coloured envelope in his hand. He gestured her into his room and she went, closing the door behind her.

'You got one as well, I believe?' He grinned as he wagged the envelope in front of her then cast it on the desk.

She nodded, her eyes lingering on his tall figure, the light blue open-neck sports shirt and the pale trousers that fitted his long legs so perfectly. She had never known him to look anything but smart in a casual way. His dark hair still looked damp and sleeked back as though he had recently showered.

She wondered, ridiculously, if he had rushed to the practice, either omitting breakfast or hurriedly eating it in the company of a female companion...and Charlotte Macdonald's face flickered briefly in her mind.

'My first reaction,' he was saying as he sat on the edge of the desk and folded his arms, 'was to telephone you yesterday. But, well, you might have had company...'

Alison nodded slowly. 'Yes, I did as a matter of fact. The same thought occurred to me. That you might be…busy.'

He bit the edge of his lip, his brown eyes glimmering as he glanced down at the floor. When he met her gaze again, he said quickly. 'Well, is it a yes or no, Ali?'

'To Annabelle Reid's invitation?'

'She's asked us to take Gem,' he said stiffly. 'Does that make any difference to you?'

Alison felt herself growing hot under her summer dress and wished that she had come to a decision before arriving here. Last night, she had thought, Why not? After talking to Clare, there had seemed little harm in it and a positive upside for Gem. Then this morning she had been filled with doubt once more and she had decided against it.

But now, looking at Sam, attempting to say no was harder than she had anticipated. Instead, she shook her head and closed her eyes. 'I don't suppose we can refuse.' She sighed deeply, opening her eyes and shrugging. 'It would seem very rude if we did.'

'So…we're agreed. We go.'

'Yes, why not?'

He gazed at her for some while, then walked to the door and leaned his shoulder against it.

'You know, it may not be so bad, Ali. Both of us need a break and this place does sound rather special. On the whole, I think it might work very well.'

'Let's hope so,' Alison said positively, more positively than she really felt, her emotions too mixed to know whether she was doing the right thing or not. 'And...Sam...that business about the asthma clinic?'

For a moment his expression became guarded. 'What of it?'

She drew her hair from her face and looked up at him. 'You have my support.'

There was no mistaking the delight in his eyes. 'What changed your mind?'

'Thomas, I think. If one asthmatic can be helped, then either it's a great coincidence or a technique that really does work.'

She was about to move when he stopped her, cupping her shoulder in his hand. She felt the warmth of his palm travel through her, snaking through her body and down into her legs. She stood immobile as he bent and brushed her cheek softly with his mouth. 'I really do appreciate that, Ali,' he murmured huskily, his breath softly dancing on her skin.

She smiled hesitantly, gulping in a breath. It was then she knew she had no control whatsoever on the emotions he could arouse in her. He hadn't kissed her for so long, she couldn't remember when it last was that he did. And this wasn't even a proper kiss but a mere thank you. But nothing had changed in the chemistry. As always, he had the power to turn her blood to fire with an ease that both shocked and frightened her.

It seemed like years before she finally came back to reality. As though that kiss had propelled her back into their past with a force that she could not recover from. And though she had long since given up trying to stop the memories from coming, her body and mind froze in self-defence mode as she forced herself to straighten her spine and step back.

'I…I'd better go,' she heard herself mumbling, and grabbed for the door.

Her hand collided with Sam's and the shock of physical contact was too much for her traumatised body. She made her escape, her legs trembling as she ascended the stairs.

In her room, she went to the window, inhaling the fresh air that drifted in from the river. She stood there, attempting to calm herself.

She told herself this was a natural reaction. A symptom of a disease that she had found remission from but not entirely cured. She had to be content with that. And she was.

Then with a sigh that came from somewhere very deep and dark inside her, she turned to her desk and, thank God, to the unfailing distraction of work.

It was the following week, at Kennet Health Centre, that Alison thought she saw Charlotte Macdonald again.

She had just left Gemma at the crèche and was walking to her room along the bright, carpeted hallway when a small figure in white appeared. She was carrying medical notes and had her dark head down. Alison's heart leapt as she stared at the figure coming towards her.

Suddenly, however, there was a tap on her shoulder and Alison turned to find Gemma's nursery nurse breathlessly holding out a set of keys. 'Dr Stewart, Gemma had these in her dungaree pocket. I thought they might be for the car.'

Alison accepted them, knowing at once that they were the keys to her old car which Gemma had been playing with earlier that morning.

'Oh, thank you, Susie,' Alison said distract-edly. 'She must have pocketed them before we left. They belong to my old car.'

'Oh, well, thought I'd better return them in case.'

Alison nodded and watched the young girl hurry back in the direction from which she had come. By the time she turned round, the hall was empty. There were three doors to her left and several to her right and a staircase leading to the first floor. Alison was tempted to go up them, but she knew her first patient was wait-ing in Reception.

When she got to her room, Alison was al-most convinced that the person she had seen couldn't possibly be Charlotte Macdonald. Why should she be here at Kennet when, as far as Alison knew, she had been a trainee nurse and had been working only temporarily in the area when she had met Sam?

That still didn't stop part of her mind from playing on the young woman in the hall, and by the time two o'clock came she had decided to approach Susie on the subject.

As Alison entered the large room that served as the practice crèche, she saw Susie and Gemma through the swing doors, still playing outside on the swings.

It was a warm but overcast July day and Gemma and another little girl were busy climbing on the small rope frame. Susie was watching them and when she saw Alison approach she smiled, glancing at her watch.

'Two o'clock already,' she remarked as Alison came to stand beside her. 'Are you going to the park today, Dr Stewart?'

'Yes, I think so, Susie.' Alison liked Susie Hall, a pleasant, fair-haired twenty-year-old who had taken care of Gemma since the beginning of the year when she had first started at the crèche. 'What about you?'

'Oh, I don't finish till four. Then I'll go home and collapse.' Susie grinned. 'I'll go and fetch her for you—'

'Susie, before you do...I was wondering if you know the staff here very well?'

Susie frowned, then shrugged. 'Well, I've only been here since January, Dr Stewart.'

'It's just that I thought I saw someone I knew,' Alison said quickly. 'But I didn't get chance to speak to them.'

'Was it one of the doctors?' Susie asked. 'We had two new ones start last week.'

'No, it was a nurse.'

'District or practice?' Susie looked curiously at Alison and for a moment Alison hesitated.

She wouldn't like this conversation to be repeated if it had been Charlotte Macdonald she'd seen.

'At the time she was a trainee midwife. Her name was Charlotte Macdonald.'

Susie's frown didn't disappear and Alison saw no flicker of recognition. Then the young nursery nurse looked down and sucked on her lip. 'That name does ring a bell. But I'm not very familiar with the midwifery team. However, Macdonald… I do recall that name from my last practice, but I was only there a month, filling in for someone, before I got transferred here.'

'And where was that?' Alison asked.

'A group practice of four doctors near Oxford. Between Oxford and Lamstone, actually.'

'I see,' Alison remarked, trying not to sound as shocked as she felt. 'Oh, well, thanks Susie. I'm sure it couldn't have been the person I knew.'

'You could ask at Reception,' Susie suggested quickly. 'Coral, the practice manager, knows everyone on the nursing teams and support staff.'

'Yes, thanks, Susie, I might do that.' Alison smiled. 'Now, I'd better try to persuade

Gemma to come with me. She looks as though she's having too much fun to leave.'

Susie laughed, and as Alison gathered Gemma and her things she hoped that Susie hadn't wondered why she was so interested in Charlotte Macdonald. Not that it really mattered. She had no real interest in identifying the woman who had wrecked her marriage. It was a subject best left alone, although that was rather difficult since twice in the space of two months Alison had thought she had seen her.

As she walked with Gemma in the buggy to the park, Alison found it difficult to recall the young and attractive woman with whom Sam had spent the night. She had met her several times, but only in a work situation. At eight months pregnant with Gemma, she had called rarely at the surgery, her own career on hold at the end of her pregnancy.

The young trainee midwife had caught her eye briefly, once as she'd sat with Sam in the office and another time, when Alison had arrived, Charlotte's petite figure looking so relaxed—and unpregnant, as she'd sat in the chair by his desk.

She'd had no suspicions then, of course. A slight flare of jealousy perhaps as Sam had sung her praises. And just before Gemma had come along, how she had been assigned to work with Sam on some of the more involved cases.

Alison realised they had arrived at the park and, going in through the gate, stopped the buggy for Gemma. Her tiny figure dashed to the edge of the paddling pool and Alison followed, spreading a towel over the grass.

Answering Gemma's excited babble of questions, Alison changed her into her swimming costume. After applying a generous coating of sunscreen, she watched her scramble into the shallow water.

She was such a beautiful child, as Sam had remarked. Legs that were already sturdy and losing their chubbiness would, no doubt, become long and gangly as the years progressed. Blonde curls trailing down her back...

Alison's heart clenched as she watched.

How could Sam have risked all this, their entire happiness, for a one-night fling? But what if it wasn't? a small voice asked inside. What if it was more than fleeting madness and Sam was in love with Charlotte Macdonald?

CHAPTER EIGHT

ON SUNDAY, the sun was masked by a cloudy sky that threatened rain. As Alison had no plans for taking Gemma out, she decided to call at the newsagent in the village, then stop at Clare's on her way home.

Swapping shorts for white trousers and cotton top, Alison curled her blonde hair up into a clip, dressed Gemma in pretty blue smock dress and told her they were off to see Aunty Clare.

Gemma, as always delighted to see her aunt, gurgled in delight when Alison gave way to temptation and also bought ice cream. A few minutes later, Alison turned the corner of her sister's road.

The house and surrounding ground had been their grandparents' and had been handed on to their mother and father in the seventies. Her father had turned the small holding into a market garden and it was here Clare and Alison had grown up.

As Alison parked in the drive, she had a fleeting memory of her mother carrying a tray of bedding plants. She had always worn trousers, jumpers and garden gloves—a tall, slim woman who had loved her two daughters to distraction...

Perhaps because she had been lost in thoughts of her childhood, Alison didn't see the dark blue car parked in the gravel car park adjacent to the house.

'Ali, Gemma...this is a surprise!' Clare exclaimed. Dressed in jeans and T-shirt, Clare had muddy stains on her clothes and Alison frowned.

'Are you working?'

'No—well, yes. Robbie's had a delivery of stone paving. For the Japanese garden.'

'How's it coming along?' Alison enquired, recalling the new innovation that Robbie had been working on all summer.

'Slowly.' Clare smiled as she bent down to scoop Gemma into her arms. She stood back to allow Alison into the house. 'You didn't say you were coming this morning.'

'I've brought the newspaper and a Sunday morning treat. Can you stop for five minutes?' Alison rummaged in her shoulder-bag and brought out both the newspaper and the ice cream.

'Oh…that looks nice.' Clare led the way through to the kitchen which, as usual, was filled with pots and tubs that trailed out into the conservatory beyond, plants and flowers of all kinds that would duly find their way into the nursery.

'Is Robbie around?' Alison asked as Clare led Gemma into the conservatory and, sinking down onto the rattan chair, lifted her niece onto her knees.

'Yes, he is. Actually, Ali—'

'I'm not stopping,' Alison said, as she wondered if she had come at an awkward time. The nursery was busy on Sundays and her sister and her husband often worked until late. 'Clare, are you all right?'

'Yes, fine… It's just that…'

Alison saw colour fill her sister's face, then turned to follow Clare's gaze as she glanced at the door and the person entering. At that moment Gemma wriggled off Clare's lap and ran towards the tall, bronzed man dressed only in shorts.

At first Alison thought it was Robbie, but took a breath as she saw it was Sam.

'Da-ddee,' cried Gemma, throwing herself into his arms. His big hands went around her and propelled her into the air.

'How's my best girl?' He held her aloft in his muscular brown arms.

Alison glanced at Clare who attempted a small shrug and stood up. 'Sam's giving Robbie some help with the patio,' she explained 'Our deadline is for opening it next week.'

'Hi.' Sam grinned at Alison.

'Hello, Sam,' Alison floundered. Looking at Clare, she added, 'Will it be ready in time?'

'With Sam's help, yes,' Clare answered quickly.

'Why don't you come and see?' Sam invited, still holding Gemma in his arms.

'Perhaps another time,' Alison murmured, glancing at Clare. 'I really can't stop—'

'Of course you can.' Clare smiled, sliding her arm through Ali's. 'Come on, we'll take some ice cream with us and sit by the pool. It will be good PR. Our customers will see there's interest already.'

'I'll take Gem on ahead if you like.' Sam's dark eyes met Ali's. 'She'll like the koi. Robbie and I have just put them in from the main tank.'

Alison tried to disengage her eyes, at the same time unable to think of a reason why she shouldn't stay. Gently lowering Gemma to the floor, Sam took her small hand and they disappeared into the garden.

'Before you say a thing,' Clare said hurriedly as Alison turned to her, 'I was going to tell you Sam was here, but—'

'How long has he been helping you?' Alison asked abruptly.

'Since Robbie's accident, actually,' Clare said, going pink. 'We should never have got the fish pool done without his help.'

'But why didn't you mention it, Clare?'

Her sister looked at her for some while before replying. 'I felt you wouldn't have approved,' she said eventually.

'Why not?'

'Because... Oh, Ali...' Clare stopped, chewing on her lip. 'You simply can't stop being friends with someone you've known for years and who's been part of the family.' She added in a rush, 'And even if Sam did have a one-night stand with that girl, it was a mistake he's paid dearly for.'

'Clare, you're supposed to be on my side,' Alison replied abruptly.

Clare came slowly towards her. Sliding her arms around her, she gave her a hug. 'Of course I'm on your side. It's just that Robbie and I were desperate—you know how things have been for us. Last year we even thought of closing. Sam offered his help and it seemed too good an offer to refuse. But I put off telling you because I didn't want to upset you.'

Alison sat down on a kitchen chair. 'It was just a shock, seeing him here.'

Clare sat beside her. 'If I was married to Sam and he'd had a fling, I would probably be feeling the same as you right now.' She paused. 'But he's not like Dad. Sam didn't deceive you for months on end, then disappear. In fact, I still find it hard to believe Sam would go astray, even for one night.'

'I don't know for certain that it was just once, Clare.'

'Don't you think you should have asked him?'

'No,' Alison replied stiffly, 'at the time I didn't.'

'But there may have been reasons—' Clare began, but stopped as Alison's head jerked up.

'Reasons for an affair?' Alison demanded.

'No…' Clare hesitated. 'But perhaps Sam thought you'd lost interest in him. You did have that awful depression—'

'Are you saying my depression was the cause of it all?'

'No,' Clare replied slowly, 'but it could have contributed.'

'I needed Sam more than ever after Gemma was born,' Alison breathed. 'but we seemed unable to communicate.'

'Maybe...' Clare murmured, looking away, 'Sam needed reassurance, too. He was, after all, the focus of your life before Gem.'

'Whatever happened between us, Clare,' Alison returned quickly, 'it wasn't a reason for Sam to stray.'

'I can't argue with that,' Clare said. Turning her attention to the ice cream, she divided the block up into dishes and placed them on a tray. Alison helped, placing spoons and cold drinks beside them, but as she accompanied Clare into the garden she couldn't help feeling dismayed and slightly abandoned, despite Clare's assertions of loyalty.

'Pretty, aren't they?' Sam twirled a long brown finger into the water of the pool that Robbie had created for his Japanese garden. The water lilies were in full bloom and the large, stately fish swam beneath, a glimmer of gold and silver catching on the surface like stars.

'It's beautiful here,' Alison murmured as she stood by the pool. The garden was filled with leafy fronds, azaleas and exotic shrubs. An energetic waterfall sparkled over rocks and boulders that Sam and Robbie had hauled into place.

'You sound surprised,' Sam replied quietly.

'I am,' she answered, frowning. 'I knew you were helping Robbie with the greenhouses, but you didn't mention you were going on to do all this.'

'What would you have said if I had?'

'I would have been pleased for Robbie...'

'That's not what I asked.'

'I...I don't know,' she began, only to be halted as one dark eyebrow shot up.

'I can guarantee that if I told you I was spending time here, you would have thought I had some sinister motive—'

'Oh, come on, Sam, now you're being silly.'

'Am I? I'm sorry, Ali, but I don't think so.'

When at last the silence became too much, Alison sank down on the stone seat at the edge of the pool. 'This is getting us nowhere, Sam,' she said quietly.

'I know,' he agreed as gales of laughter rose from the other end of the pool where Robbie and Clare were playing with Gemma.

'That should be us,' Sam murmured as he followed her gaze.

She looked back at him. 'It was once, wasn't it?'

'Then let's draw a line under it all,' he said softly. 'I know it won't ever be the same. That you and I are now leading different lives. But it shouldn't take too much effort for us to behave like loving parents.'

Alison noted the cold words and took in a breath. Loving parents, yes, the little voice inside her repeated. But not lovers...

Unintentional though it was, Sam seemed to edge closer. And despite her efforts to compose herself, her eyes kept sliding to the grainy brown skin of his legs and the ebony hair that covered them. She had forgotten how long and sinewy they were. Aware of the reaction he was causing, she leaned down and studied the pool.

When he sank beside her, she swallowed dryly.

'I should have put a pond in the garden,' he murmured, his long brown fingers rippling the water.

She smiled shakily. 'I'm not certain I'd trust Gemma yet.'

'No, perhaps not for a couple of years. Now, a swimming pool might be a better idea.

Somewhere for Gem to bring her friends. Then I can keep an eye on her.'

'And incite a rebellion?' Alison laughed, though she knew he was half-serious and thinking of Victoria Reid.

He sat round on the stone seat and spread his long body casually over it. 'Didn't we all rebel at fourteen?'

Alison pushed herself up from the edge of the pond. 'There wasn't the need, in my case.'

He groaned softly. 'Oh, God, Ali, I forgot. Your dad left home then.'

'Yes, Dad was the rebel. Not me.'

He was silent for a moment, deep in thought. 'That was tough,' he sighed eventually.

'Tougher for Mum,' Alison glanced at the end of the pool. 'But when she died, I think she had no regrets. Not even over Dad.'

Sam frowned. 'And what about you, Ali? Have you ever come to terms with him leaving?'

She looked at him then and shrugged. 'I accepted it,' she said quietly.

He held her gaze and it was then that Alison knew she must leave. Calling Gemma, she stood up.

'Will you be in later?' he asked, as he stood beside her. 'I was, er, thinking of calling on my way home—to say goodnight to Gem.'

She would normally have agreed, but on impulse she shook her head. 'Not tonight, Sam. Perhaps during the week?'

Whatever it was he was thinking, he made no reply and it was during the drive home that Alison felt guilty for having refused his request.

Should she have made an effort? As she lifted Gemma from the car seat and put her to bed for her midday nap, the cottage seemed oddly empty. Sitting in the lounge, she browsed the newspapers. But soon she gave herself up to the thoughts that monopolised her mind.

Her heart gave a traitorous leap as she recalled Sam today, naked to the waist, his tanned shoulders and strong arms so familiar that she recalled every inch of honed muscle, the sprinkling of dark hair that snaked down to the belt of his shorts, the damp streak that glimmered at his spine, his deeply tanned skin that stretched over his bones like silk. And those haunting brown eyes—eyes that always seemed to look inside her, to the very places she attempted to hide.

Memories crowded in. Their love-making, the deep and sensual fulfilment of their passion. True to his character, Sam had no inhibitions about the act of love. And though he hadn't been her first boyfriend, he had been her first love. He had taught her to cast off any preconceptions she might have had about giving. She had given to him completely, learning to trust.

Where had their love gone? She ached to know as her heart squeezed and she rebuked herself for the self-torment.

Then, as she heard Gemma's soft murmurings upstairs, she comforted herself with the thought that at least on one level their love had endured, in the child they had created. And for whom she must forget the past and learn to exist in some other way.

On Friday of the following week, Eila Hayward returned to the surgery. This time there was a marked deterioration in her health. She had lost a worrying amount of weight and complained of difficulty in sleeping. 'I'm tired during the day,' she explained, looking pale and gaunt. 'I fall into bed at night, and then wake up even before Anthony.'

'How is he sleeping?' Alison asked as Eila turned down the cover that snugly fitted the buggy and revealed Anthony's dark head.

'Occasionally, he'll go through the night. And that awful nappy rash has cleared up.'

'Well, let's have a quick look at you.' Alison examined Eila and satisfied herself that there was nothing obviously wrong. 'Are you breastfeeding?' she asked as Eila buttoned up her blouse.

'I supplement with the bottle,' Eila responded. 'I don't seem to have enough to satisfy him. The health visitor says he's bonny enough and that I shouldn't worry, but I do. I can't settle to anything either, though goodness knows there's so much to be done in the house…'

'Well, Anthony looks fine to me,' Alison replied encouragingly as she glanced at the sleeping baby. Then she looked at Eila. 'Have you lost more weight?'

Her patient shrugged. 'I haven't got the same appetite.'

'Do you eat a meal each day?'

Eila looked down at her hands. 'I try to. But sometimes Mark can't manage to get home. He's very busy with his football and…'

Alison waited for her to continue, but saw that tears filled her eyes. Eila drew out a handkerchief and blew her nose, then lifted her shoulders in a shrug.

'How about family help? Someone you could leave the baby with for a few hours? Your mother or mother-in-law?' Alison probed gently.

'We don't live near my mother and Mark's parents died. I do have a sister, but she lives in Scotland. And to be honest, I wouldn't like to leave Anthony. I have this worry that something is going to happen to him.'

Alison soon became aware that the responsibility for Anthony was what was at the root of Eila's problem. For some women their new role caused a deep internal upheaval. It was eased if the problem could be discussed with their partners, but in this case Alison felt that it was not so.

With another pang of sympathy for Eila she recalled her own anxiety, which had led to depression after Gemma's birth. How she longed to talk to Sam about her feelings but had felt too ashamed of them to do so. Added to which, Sam had worked long hours, which had left them little time to be together.

'Try not to worry about those feelings,' she attempted to explain, but could see by her patient's weary response that her words were falling on stony ground. 'You may be suffering from depression—'

Eila sat up in her seat. 'Anthony is the best thing that's happened to me,' she blurted out.

'I'm certain he is,' Alison replied calmly. 'And many new mums feel as you do. The anxiety will gradually fade but, should the problem continue, I can prescribe you something to help. Meanwhile, you do need to rest to compensate for your lack of sleep. Is there no one who could sit with Anthony in the daytime?'

Eila shrugged. 'I'm out of touch with my friends. None of them have babies yet. I could ask my neighbour. But I don't like to trouble her. I don't really know her well enough.'

'You need to turn off,' Alison persisted. 'Just for a few hours at least. Even if you can't sleep, you must try to rest.'

Standing up, Eila smiled. 'Easier said than done, Dr Stewart, but I'll try.'

Alison watched her leave, sadly aware that she had been unable to help.

At the end of the day, Lucy stopped her in Reception. 'I saw Eila here earlier,' the young receptionist said curiously. 'She's lost so much weight. I hope there's nothing really wrong.'

'She's very isolated after having the baby,' Alison replied, unable to discuss her patient's problems. 'I understand there's no family near.'

'Isn't there?' Lucy sighed. 'That must be awful. I don't know what I would do without my mum and sisters.' She frowned. 'I'd call, but I don't want her to think I'm poking my nose in.'

'As it happens, I think she would appreciate it, Lucy,' Alison said at once, wondering if it was Lucy that Eila had been referring to when she'd mentioned a neighbour.

'Do you? Well, after I've given my other half his tea tonight, I'll pop round.'

'I shouldn't like her to think I've been discussing her visit,' Alison said quickly.

Lucy smiled and nodded. 'No problem. I'm always running out of stuff and I've asked to borrow milk before now. I'll let you know how I get on, Dr Stewart.'

Grateful to Lucy for her help, Alison was still thinking about Eila as she returned to her room. But before she got there, she found Hector and Sam standing in the hall.

'Just the person I wanted to see,' Hector said with a charming grin. 'I wonder, do you ride, Ali? Sam tells me you do.'

It took a few moments before Alison realised what he was driving at. Blushing slightly, she glanced at Sam. 'Does this have a connection to the bank holiday weekend?' she asked cautiously.

'It does indeed.' Hector nodded. 'Annie has some astonishing mounts and will organise a small jaunt if you're up for it.'

'I haven't ridden for years,' Alison said at once. 'Not since our last holiday.' Again she looked at Sam.

'Yes...four years,' Sam agreed, his eyes suddenly reflective. 'We found a gorgeous beach in Cornwall and a riding stable nearby. We rode nearly all week. It was a fantastic holiday.'

His words brought back the memory of the seven short but heavenly days they had spent in a seaside cottage, entirely alone. Except, of course, for the horses, splashing along the shore in the early morning and at sunset. Yes, those were the best times, with the sky full of fire and the wonderful fresh air filling their lungs. And then, at the end of the day, a panorama spreading out before them as they stood on the balcony of the cottage. The scent of the sea and the sand drifting into the bedroom...Sam's arms lifting her onto the cool sheets, their bodies radiating the sun and the water as they made love.

'Ali?' She jumped as Sam's voice broke into her consciousness.

'Sorry,' she mumbled. 'What was that?'

'I was telling Hector about Cornwall,' he said. 'The point being, Annie would like to know if we ride.'

'Well, yes...' Alison hesitated. 'But what about Gem?'

'I'm certain it's not beyond Annie and I to keep her amused.' Hector chuckled.

Alison glanced at Sam then back at Hector. 'I suppose there's no harm...'

'That's the spirit, Ali.' Hector patted Alison's shoulder. 'I'll tell Annie you're up for a jaunt. Now, must dash, I'm running late.'

Alison and Sam were both silent as Hector disappeared down the hall. Sam took Alison's arm and led her into her room.

'I engineered none of that,' he said with genuine concern.

'I didn't think you did,' Alison replied with a sigh.

'Hector caught me off guard—I wondered what he was getting at.'

'Has he asked Peter yet?'

Sam nodded. 'I have to admit, Hector is going all out to make this a memorable occasion.'

Alison smiled despite herself. 'Yes, it might be fun…'

Sam's eyes widened. 'Do you think so?'

'Yes—it sounds like a perfect weekend.'

'It didn't really start out that way, did it?' he murmured, his head slightly bent in surprise. And though his mouth was turned down slightly, she found herself captivated by the deeply tanned skin and shock of dark hair that grew so thickly over his scalp. She wondered if Gemma's hair would darken as she grew older. Alison looked into the glistening brown pools of Gemma's eyes and her heart gave that exquisite jump. A guilty pang followed and she forced herself to smile, hopefully hiding her thoughts.

'No, it didn't,' she agreed as she lifted her bag from the chair and switched off her computer. She came to stand beside him. 'But I want to make this work, Sam. Living apart and raising our daughter can work, but only if we make the effort.' A remark that brought only a brief nod as they said goodnight.

*   *   *

Sam arrived to see Gemma on Saturday. They spent a few hours in the garden, but he was on call that evening and left at five. It had been a pleasant enough visit, Alison reflected afterwards, and Gemma had fallen asleep contented and happy.

Which was, of course, the whole purpose of him calling, she mused as she showered before bed. He hadn't referred to their conversation and she wondered if now they could possibly have arrived at some understanding.

Sleep came with difficulty. Although she tried to read, her thoughts were too scattered to concentrate. When at last she turned out the light, she lay awake, the doubts as ever tumbling through her mind. One day, her reasonable self said, Gemma will be old enough to spend time alone with Sam—a day not far off. Where would he take her? And with whom?

It was a thought that niggled so insistently she was forced to sit up and switch on the light again. The irony of it was, she had made it clear they were to lead separate lives. But despite all her reasoning, the thought of Sam and Gemma and this other person, whoever it was, distressed her.

She had wanted to establish a civilised relationship and now it seemed she had succeeded. But for all the satisfaction it gave her, she was back at square one. A fact that was brought home to her as she wondered who would be waiting for Sam whilst he was on call and who he returned home to tonight.

CHAPTER NINE

IT WAS a Monday at the end of July when Alison attended the first of Sam's asthma clinics. She had referred a patient of her own, a young woman with a history of mild asthma. Kerry Ames was nineteen and taking a year out of her studies to teach English on the Continent.

'I've been trying not to use my bronchodilator,' Kerry had told Alison the previous week. 'I'm not dependent on it, but would rather not use it at all.'

This remark had prompted Alison to suggest Sam's clinic, and Kerry had agreed.

The slim, brown-haired young woman sat with three other asthmatics in the large airy room on the ground floor normally reserved for practice meetings and staff social gatherings.

The sight of four adults all holding their breath caused Hector, who sat next to Alison at the back of the room, to smile. 'I'd never have believed it if I hadn't seen it myself,' he whispered, and Alison nodded.

'Nor me. It was Sam's success with Thomas Knight that was impressive.'

'The principle is shallow breathing?' Hector murmured.

'It's a little more complicated than that, I believe,' Alison replied. 'But Sam explained that when asthma attacks happen, you increase your rate of overbreathing or hyperventilation. If you know how to control your hyperventilation, you can overcome an attack.'

'In other words, if you can normalise your breathing, you can cure your asthma?' Hector nodded slowly. 'That's a pretty revolutionary idea to take on board.'

'Yes. But my patient Kerry Ames, the young woman sitting next to Thomas, was willing to try it and I agreed. When she arrived this evening she was wheezing, so perhaps it was quite opportune that she attended.'

After the hour was over, Kerry came over and sat beside Alison.

'How are you feeling, Kerry?' she asked immediately.

'I did the exercises,' Kerry replied, clearly delighted. 'And I controlled my wheeze.' She lifted her shoulders in a shrug. 'It's wonderful not to resort to the bronchodilator.'

'Will we see you tomorrow?'

Kerry nodded. 'It's a five-day course. I've told Dr Stewart I'll be attending each session.'

'Well, good luck with the practising.' Alison smiled.

'One satisfied customer,' commented Hector dryly. 'Wonder if she'll maintain her improvement?'

'If she continues to practise, yes,' a deep voice said confidently, and Alison looked up to see Sam standing there.

'How were your other volunteers?' Hector asked as Sam took a seat beside them.

'Willing to learn,' Sam replied, glancing over at the group. 'The breathing technique's not a quick fix—it needs practice and understanding. As does everything worthwhile,' he added, glancing first at Alison and then back at Hector before changing the subject.

As Alison drove to Clare's that night, she couldn't forget Sam's comment, wondering whether or not it had been cryptically directed at their relationship. Perhaps it was for this reason that she answered her sister rather abruptly when Clare sang Sam's praises.

'Robbie opened the Japanese garden today,' she told Alison as they stood by the car in the warm evening sun. 'It went brilliantly, thanks to Sam's help. He's said he'd call by to see the finished product tonight. Why don't you and Gemma stay? We can all have supper.'

Alison opened the car door and lowered Gemma into her seat. 'I'm sorry, but I've someone calling this evening.'

'Oh,' Clare answered in surprise. 'Anyone I know?'

'No.' Alison smiled, unable to resist teasing Clare. 'But I'll give you a clue. He's tall, blond and in his mid-thirties.'

'Tell me more,' Clare breathed, her eyebrows shooting up.

'You'll have to wait,' Alison told her as she jumped in the car. 'I'm late already.'

'I'll ring you tomorrow,' Clare called through the open window of the car. 'But I won't forgive you for keeping secrets.'

'Look who's talking!' Alison exclaimed as she started the engine.

Her sister's curiosity was mildly amusing, Alison reflected as she drove home. But what if the male calling tonight hadn't simply been the engineer from the Aga company but someone with whom she might want to become involved?

Would there come a time when she would want to start dating? Both she and Sam would have to pick up the threads of a social life again and perhaps Sam had already done so. But there had only ever been one man in her life and she had never thought there would be anyone else for either of them.

And even after that dreadful night when Sam had turned up in the early hours with lipstick on his handkerchief and the accompanying smell of a woman's scent—even then, her numbed mind hadn't been able to take it all in. And if she was honest, it still hadn't.

The cottage garden was littered with balloons and toys. Despite the attempts to restore calm by the mothers of the four little girls who were attending Gemma's birthday party, most of the pool water had been splashed onto the grass.

Alison had decided to postpone tea until Robbie and Sam, dressed only in shorts and thongs, had filled the plastic pool afresh.

'So, who was your mystery man?' Clare asked as they watched five sets of mud-caked limbs clamber into the paddling pool.

'That would be telling.' Alison grinned as she tied her blonde hair into a ponytail and slipped on her shades. Wearing shorts and a bright pink T-shirt, she was enjoying the brief moment of relaxation on the swing seat before tea.

'Oh, come on, Ali, that's not fair.' Her sister pouted under her sunhat.

For a moment Alison paused, but she doubted whether she could lie convincingly enough to fool Clare. 'If you mean the Aga man...' She laughed. 'No, we didn't have a big seduction scene. But he did manage to put right whatever was wrong with it.'

'The Aga man?' Clare repeated disappointedly. 'You mean it wasn't a toy-boy?'

'No.' Alison grinned. 'It wasn't.'

Clare chuckled, turning to lean her elbow on the cushions. 'I never really thought it was. You're a one-man woman, Alison Stewart.'

An opinion Alison found disconcerting. Raising her voice slightly above the children's screams, she shrugged lightly. 'Perhaps I haven't found that one man yet.'

It was a comment that did nothing to impress her sister, or the dripping wet figure standing behind her. Clare looked up. 'Sam! Where did you spring from?'

Alison swivelled round on the seat.

'Am I interrupting?' he muttered, casting them both suspicious looks as he towelled the dirty water from his legs.

'Nothing special,' Alison replied quickly. 'I was about to call the children for tea.' She saw

Clare's amused glance, which did nothing to add to her composure as she avoided Sam's penetrating stare.

'Do you think he heard us?' Clare whispered when they were alone again.

'Why should it matter if he did?' Alison shrugged, sliding her eyes toward Sam's lean figure playing ball with Gemma.

'It's just...' Clare sighed, continuing their conversation as she rose and walked towards the kitchen. 'Well, I shouldn't like Robbie to have overheard something like that.'

'Robbie never strayed,' Alison answered sharply. 'And besides, why shouldn't I enjoy other men's company?'

'Because...because...' Clare lifted her shoulders exasperatedly. 'Because he would be hurt, that's why.'

'Yes, I know how that feels,' Alison replied as they stepped inside the kitchen. 'Clare, Sam is probably in a relationship himself by now— or hadn't that occurred to you?'

Her sister frowned. 'He's never said if he is.'

'I shouldn't be too certain,' Alison remarked as she lifted the birthday cake from the shelf.

'What do you mean by that?'

'Just that I thought I saw Charlotte Macdonald at the surgery,' Alison said with a dismissive shrug that immediately brought a gasp from Clare.

'You mean...the girl Sam was supposed to have had a fling with?'

Alison had always known that Clare doubted Sam's infidelity. But it was never more plain than now as she stared at her. 'But didn't you tell me she'd disappeared after Sam went to Australia?' Clare asked.

'One of the district nurses told me that, yes. Anyway, it doesn't matter,' Alison continued defensively. 'It makes no difference to me if Sam is still involved with her. For all I know, she may be the reason for his return from Australia.'

To which Clare replied in a voice that Alison recognised only too well, 'Now, if that was my husband, I'd find out what really did happen that night and not hide my head in the sand.'

A remark that Alison chose to ignore as she lit the two tiny pink candles. It was all very well for Clare to say that but it wasn't her husband who had given in to temptation. It was Sam.

*   *   *

When the candles had been blown out and all the food eaten, Clare organised a final game of pass the parcel. By five o'clock, Alison was waving off the last little girl and her mother.

'You and Robbie must stay to supper,' Alison said as Clare stood beside her at the front door. 'I'll cook something light—omelette and salad.'

'Wish we could,' Clare sighed. 'But Marge and her husband are only covering for us until six. Since the Japanese garden's been open, we seem to have people staying on in the evenings. And goodness knows, we could do with the business.'

'Perhaps another time.' Alison sighed as she watched her sister grab her sunhat and bag from the hall.

'Sam said he'll stay on to help you clear up,' Clare added as Robbie joined her.

'There's no need,' Alison replied, a little too quickly, and Clare's eyebrows rose fractionally.

'I'm sure Sam could do with feeding,' her sister added dryly, throwing her a mischievous smile.

Alison watched their car move away and returned to the kitchen, wondering if Clare had a point. Sam had been hard at work all day, helping her to prepare for the party. From the kitchen window she saw Sam on all fours, Gemma riding on his lean brown back.

Gemma was wearing her shorts and T-shirt, her plump little arms wrapped lovingly around Sam's neck. Their laughter echoed inside and for a long while Alison watched them as Sam played the clown and Gemma hung on with grim determination.

Her tiny fingers curled into his thick dark hair and finally he collapsed, bringing shrieks of laughter from Gemma. There the two of them remained, lazing in the sunshine, the golden threads of sunlight reflecting in Gemma's curls.

Occasionally she would squirm into her father's strong brown arms and his laughter rippled across to the house. The muscles of his long legs were spattered with blades of grass and his thronged feet were splashed with mud. Only his colourful shorts seemed to have survived the day unmarked, their bright colours accentuating the cloud of black hair that covered his thighs.

Alison was hungrily devouring the scene when he suddenly turned. She smiled briefly, lowering her head as though she had been busy at the sink. Her heart raced as she wondered if she should follow Clare's advice.

It would be no trouble to feed him after Gemma was asleep, she told herself quickly. Or perhaps, more sensibly, they could eat whilst Gemma was still up.

Deciding on this, Alison piled the dirty crockery into the dishwasher, then joined Sam and Gemma in the garden.

It was a beautiful, golden evening. The summer flowers were out in abundance, their blue and greens and pinks a perfect backdrop against the fruit trees.

Sam was sitting on the swing seat with Gemma beside him. 'I was wondering,' Alison asked as she sat beside Gemma, 'if you'd like to stay for supper?'

'Oh,' Sam murmured, then frowned. 'I'd like to, Ali, but I have to leave in a little while. I'm sorry—what about another evening?'

'Yes, maybe,' she said quickly, hiding her disappointment. She should be relieved since the sooner he left the quicker she could get on with the tidying up. Since he said no more, she left him with Gemma and returned to the house.

Why, she wondered, should she feel this way? After all, it had only been her intention to be polite. However, it had been an enjoyable day and she was reluctant to end it.

A few minutes later the telephone rang and Alison answered it. 'Dr Stewart, I'm sorry to disturb you, I know it's Gem's party today, but this is rather an emergency.'

'What is it, Lucy?' Alison asked as she recognised the receptionist's voice.

'It's Eila Hayward, my neighbour. She's very distressed. Mark has, well…just disappeared.'

'Are you with her?' Alison asked quickly.

'Yes, and, to be perfectly honest, I'm worried about leaving her.'

'Is Anthony all right?'

'As a matter of fact, that's what made me come round. I heard him screaming when I was in the garden and he didn't seem to stop.'

Just as Alison was about to reply she felt Sam's hand on her shoulder. 'Can I help?' he mouthed as he held Gemma in his arms.

Alison covered the mouthpiece. 'It's one of my patients. There's some sort of domestic crisis.'

'I'll stay here if you need to visit,' he told her, but Alison frowned.

'I thought you had to go?'

'It's nothing that can't wait.' He shrugged. 'This is more important.'

'Alison nodded then spoke to Lucy. 'Are you able to stay until I arrive?' she asked.

Lucy told her she would, and a few minutes later Alison had changed into cotton trousers and a cool shirt and was ready to leave.

'Bye, Mummy.' Gemma giggled as she stood with Sam on the doorstep.

'Bye,' Sam called as they waved her off. On her drive to Eila's house, Alison wondered curiously who it was that Sam would be disappointing tonight. Would they be sympathetic about the reason for his delay?

As she drew up outside Eila Hayward's semi-detached house, all seemed quiet. But when she knocked at the blue-painted door she thought she could hear a baby crying. A few seconds later Lucy opened the door with Anthony in her arms.

'Oh, thank goodness you've come, Dr Stewart,' Lucy said anxiously. 'Eila's upstairs in bed—first door on the right. I was just going to feed Anthony.'

'He sounds hungry,' Alison said as the baby began to cry again.

'I've made up a bottle,' Lucy replied. 'I'll feed him while you see Eila.'

'Is she asleep?' Alison asked as they paused in the hall.

'No, but she looks exhausted. I wouldn't be surprised if she's had a breakdown or something.'

The house was clean but it seemed to Alison as though it was neglected. Clothes and shoes were strewn untidily about and as she entered the bedroom it was in much the same state as downstairs.

Alison drew a wooden chair to the bed and Eila opened her eyes. She looked very pale and her eyes were heavily swollen with weeping. Her dark hair needed a wash and it was obvious that Eila had neglected herself for some time, as well as the house.

From the distressed answers her patient gave her, it appeared that Mark had left the house two days before during a quarrel. He had packed a bag, leaving Eila without a forwarding address.

It didn't take long before Eila became distraught. Alison administered a sedative. As she sat by the bed, the phone rang downstairs and Alison went into the hall, wondering if it might be Mark.

'That was Mary Flynn, Eila's mother,' Lucy said a few seconds later as she came up the stairs. 'I had to tell her why I was answering the phone and not Eila or Mark.'

'And what did she say?' Alison asked curiously.

'She said she'd been worried about Eila for months now and knew something was wrong. She said she'd drive over—although it might take her a good hour to get here. She said she'd feared Eila was unhappy and that their marriage had been under a strain for a long while.'

Remarks that didn't bode well for the young woman's future, thought Alison sadly.

It was half past eight when Mary Flynn arrived. After a brief discussion she assured Alison that she would stay and look after her daughter and grandson. The cracks in the marriage had apparently been evident to her even before Anthony's arrival.

Alison thanked Lucy and told Mary that although she herself wouldn't be in the surgery the following day, she would write a follow-up visit in the book for one of her colleagues.

It was dusk as Alison drove from Lamstone to Timpton, and as she entered the village, the lights from the Horse and Hat glowed warmly onto the forecourt. A few holidaymakers sat outside on benches, enjoying the last of the evening sun. The door to the pub was thrown open, letting in the air to a comfortably packed bar. It was a picturesque village scene and when Alison drove into her own road, Keys Cottage looked equally welcoming, Gemma's pink light glowing from upstairs.

Alison parked behind Sam's car, a sudden nervousness filling her. Would he be with Gemma, reading a story? It was late for her to be up but, then it had been an exceptional day.

However, when she walked in, the creak of the front door alerted no one. Alison walked through to the garden where all was tidy. Chairs, tables and pool had been removed to the wooden shed and the lawn cleared of toys. On her way back, one glance around the kitchen told her that Sam had been busy here, too.

Placing her bag in the hall, she glanced upstairs. The noise of the plumbing indicated that Sam was bathing Gemma. It was therefore surprising, once she'd climbed the stairs and over the gate, to find the bathroom empty.

As she peered around the nursery door, Alison was even more surprised to find Gemma fast asleep. She trod softly to her bedside, bent and kissed her daughter, drawing a soft murmur from Gemma's lips. Her teddy had dropped to the floor and Alison lifted it, tucking it beside her.

It was the noise of the *en suite* shower that caused her to leave the nursery and go slowly towards her bedroom. The ivory muslin curtain over the window blew gently as she entered. On the bed was a pair of light-coloured chinos and a T-shirt. A sports bag was open beside them and a shaving bag was in evidence on the big double bed.

With a start, Alison felt propelled backwards in time, her brain recording the familiar objects and the intimate atmosphere that pervaded the bedroom. Almost as though hypnotised, she found herself walking towards the bathroom. The scent that was Sam curled out with the steam, an aroma of shampoo and shower gel and the cologne that was unquestionably his.

As she pushed the door open with her fingertips, she took a breath, her eyes locked to the steamy glass directly in front of her.

Sam's tall, naked shape stood there, oblivious to her presence. His face was tilted upward to the shower. The water beat down, rippling over his long, wet body and against the glass between them.

Alison stared at his outline, masked by steam yet so powerfully familiar. At the long, tanned back and slim hips that curved into buttocks whose tight, masculine shape could not be disguised by the frosted glass.

Her heart seemed to miss a beat as she stared, watching his movements with eyes that were hungry for more, unable to look away as he raised his muscled arms upward into the flow of water.

How long she watched she didn't know. Her powers of self-control disappearing, she couldn't help herself or arrest the longing that was growing inside her as her hungry eyes absorbed each movement, each twist and turn, devouring the beauty of his agile body as he washed beneath the water.

And it was only when the shower door slid open and he shook the water from his drenched hair that she realised what she was doing. Unfortunately too late, as his eyes found hers.

'Ali?' he questioned, grasping a white towel from the rail. Curling it around his hips, he came towards her. 'Is everything all right?'

She nodded, her throat tight and dry. 'Y-yes…fine.'

'I showered in here. You don't mind, do you?'

'No. Of course not.' She hardly dared look at him. At the chiselled features and inky wet hair slicked back across his scalp. At the long, straight nose that made his profile so unique and which she had so often trailed a finger over during their love-making, drawing a line downward over his chin and throat, piercing the forest of black hair of his chest. At those eyes, now assessing her, driving into her mind with fierce concentration as she was unable to move.

'I bathed Gem,' he said quietly, 'then read her a story.'

Alison nodded, unable to form words. What was happening to her? What was she doing here? Waiting—hoping for what?

Walking into the bedroom, the knot in her stomach tightened. Her senses felt confused, overpowered by the power of his presence. The soft glow of the bedside table reflected on his wet skin. His broad shoulders steamed slightly, their honed muscle like brown marble, glimmering in the light. She longed to reach out, touch him, trail her fingers across them and into the damp, glistening forest of hair beneath.

'I…didn't know…when you'd be back,' he said huskily, watching her. His touch was so light that she stood without murmur as his hand slid gently to her neck and released the clip from her hair. 'I prefer it loose,' he whispered, almost too low for her to hear. 'You have such beautiful hair, Ali…like pale silk.'

'Sam…' She tried to talk, but couldn't continue. She was transfixed by what his fingers were doing, tunnelling in her hair, gently playing with the strands as they fell around her neck.

He groaned softly, a deep, smothered sound from low in his chest as he moved towards her. His hand slid down to her hip and she didn't resist as he pulled her towards him.

His kiss was long and slow, but there was nothing that could disguise his need as he drew her more firmly against him. He groaned again, this time holding her head with his other hand, his tongue snaking out to fiercely part her lips.

An anguished reply slid from her throat as she curled her arms around his neck, giving way to the pressure of his hand.

'This is what you do to me, Ali,' he moaned, as his tongue teased her mouth and another little cry of pleasurable pain escaped her lips. 'I want you, Ali, want you more than anything in this world.'

She looked into his eyes, her heart beating so violently in her chest she barely caught his words. She slid her hands to the smooth, wet shoulders that felt so strong beneath her touch. Her body ached for him, needed him and cried out for his touch.

Before she could speak, his fingers were undoing her shirt and slipping in, finding her breasts and caressing them so that she hardly dared to breathe. It had been so long, such a tortuous age since he had touched her. He was bending then and suddenly she found herself lying on the bed, his arm across her and his mouth teasing the aching peak below her shirt.

Nothing seemed to matter then, only how he touched her and kissed her. She closed her eyes as he slid off her shirt and undid the waistband of her trousers, drawing them over her legs. They fell to the floor, soon to be joined by her bra and panties, and she lay there, suddenly self-conscious of her nakedness.

'You haven't changed, Ali. You're the most beautiful woman,' he breathed, his fingertips teasing their way over her breasts. His naked body shuddered beside her, the white towel cast aside. Her hungry eyes feasted again on the graceful lines of his body.

Her breath caught in her throat as she realised she was lying beneath him, his body over her, and she met his eyes again, those dark, deep brown eyes that seemed to drown her...

'Ali...for God's sake, stop me now...if this isn't what you want,' he whispered. Lifting one hand, he laid his palm against her face, his eyes questioning.

It was impossible to refuse him.

She wanted him as much as he wanted her. More perhaps. The truth was she had no power to stop what was happening but it was as he kissed her again that she suddenly realised what might happen as a result of their lovemaking. What if she became pregnant? What would happen then? To her, to Gemma...?

She stiffened, the enormity of what they were doing suddenly clear in her need-crazed mind. How could she make love to him when they weren't a family? When their lives had been split apart by Sam's selfish actions and from which her life and Gemma's had suffered so desperately?

Appalled by her own actions, she stared into the face that moments ago had held her spellbound. He was quick to see the doubt in her eyes and for a moment she felt him shudder as a deep sigh travelled up through his body.

He rolled slowly beside her and for a moment he lay there, his body tense as he searched her face. Her body still ached for him, craved him, and yet the look in his eyes now told her his question had been answered.

Reaching out, he drew the sheet over her. Then he sat up, girding his naked hips with the towel. He regarded her steadily, as she, too, slipped forward on the bed and gathered her clothes from the floor.

'Ali,' he grated as she stood up, 'Ali…wait.'

'In a moment,' she heard herself mumble as she sought the safety of the bathroom. Once inside it, she sat down on the stool, attempting to compose her shaking body. For some while she tried not to think at all, for she knew she would make no sense of what had happened.

She dressed slowly and splashed cold water on her face, avoiding her reflection in the mirror. She didn't want to see the hidden yearning in her eyes. Or the remains of the desire that had caused him to try to make love to her.

She couldn't blame this on him.

She had wanted him with equal need, a passion that had overwhelmed her common sense and even the pain of his infidelity.

Alison straightened and, opening the door of the bathroom, her heart raced crazily as she looked into the bedroom. There was only the unmade bed, the crumpled sheets and the hollow echo of silence.

The same empty silence that now gripped her heart.

CHAPTER TEN

IT WAS the following day that Alison came face to face with Charlotte Macdonald.

Perhaps because she had been dreading seeing Sam, she didn't at first recognise the young woman sitting in the practice office, talking to Pam.

'Oh, Dr Stewart,' Pam said as she rose from the desk, 'this is Charlotte Macdonald. She used to work on our nursing team—midwifery.'

Charlotte stood up, her dark eyes curiously meeting Alison's. Although Alison recalled a slim, attractive girl with short dark hair, she was now looking at a heavily pregnant young woman, and it was a few moments before she realised who it was.

'Hello, Dr Stewart,' she said immediately. Coming towards Alison, she frowned. 'I don't know if you remember me. I met you before you had your baby—a little girl, wasn't it?'

Stunned, Alison stood without replying, her eyes unable to leave the girl's face.

'You've probably forgotten me,' the girl continued. 'I was in my last year of training. A couple of years back—perhaps not quite that much. And it was your husband who helped me on that dreadful night... If it wasn't for him I should have given up nursing altogether.'

Alison frowned at the young woman who was standing in front of her, calmly talking about Sam. The same young woman whose lipstick and scent she had found on Sam's handkerchief and over which they had had that final, explosive quarrel before he'd walked out.

At that precise moment the door opened and Sam entered. There seemed to be a breathless pause as he stood there, his eyes flicking briefly across the room and meeting Alison's. Then he turned and with a slow smile of recognition held out his hand to greet Charlotte.

She grasped it and he shook it warmly. 'Dr Stewart, I was just talking to your wife...'

But before he could reply, Pam interrupted. 'Here's your list, Dr Stewart. I have to start my shift in Reception.' She turned slightly. 'Bye, Charlotte. It was nice seeing you again.'

After she left Sam said quickly, 'So, Charlotte, tell me...how did the new job go?'

'Brilliantly,' Charlotte said at once. 'You were absolutely right. Coming out of midwifery wasn't the end of the world. There's a crèche provided, too, for the university staff. And my post as health adviser to the students, though nowhere as hands-on as midwifery, is a wonderful challenge.'

'I'm glad it worked out for the best,' Sam said pleasantly, but there was a coolness in his eyes as he turned back to Alison. 'This young lady had the misfortune to develop epilepsy in her final year of nursing.'

'I was desperately worried,' Charlotte continued eagerly, 'about my career, and had it not been for your husband helping me that night I don't know what I would have done.'

'Good sense would have prevailed eventually,' Sam said quietly.

But Charlotte shook her head. 'Not before I had done something irresponsible like crash my car or put someone at risk, as I almost did that night.' She glanced at Alison. 'You see, I'd had two previous attacks and couldn't bring myself to tell my nursing superior. I loved my job and couldn't bear the thought of losing it. I'd worked so hard to become a midwife and epilepsy would have meant that unless the seizures were very well controlled, I'd have to give it up.'

Alison heard herself respond in a voice she barely recognised. 'So it was because of your epilepsy that my husband stayed with you?'

Charlotte gave a short laugh. 'Why, yes, of course. If Dr Stewart hadn't arrived and performed the delivery in time, and then spent all those hours talking some sense into me...well, heaven knows what would have happened. I could have put that woman's life at risk—and the baby's, too.'

'But you did seek treatment,' Sam said quietly.

'Yes, thanks to you, I did, Dr Stewart. And now I'm taking anticonvulsant drugs, I can control the seizures. But as I told you when I last saw you, nursing isn't an option for me now. I'd never relax, knowing that any moment I might have a fit. That's why I asked you for a reference. I went back to further education and when the job came up as health adviser at the university, I was determined to go for it.'

For a moment the room seemed very still and no one spoke until Charlotte walked towards Alison and smiled softly 'I'm glad we met again, Dr Stewart. I owe so much to your husband.'

If the silence that had preceded her departure had been uncomfortable, the one that followed it was almost unbearable. As she stood alone with Sam, Alison realised that even if Charlotte had been a first-rate actress and had managed to offset an unpleasant encounter by some very quick thinking, it didn't explain the way Sam had handled the past few minutes in the way he had.

She knew him well enough to know that his empathy towards the girl was genuine but—and here was the crunch—held no sexual overtones. Neither had his enquiries as to her work, or the characteristically modest way in which he'd explained Charlotte's epilepsy and his part in helping her.

But as this realisation dawned, so did another. If Sam had spent the night with Charlotte in completely innocent circumstances, why hadn't he tried harder to convince her of the truth during that terrible quarrel or in the time they'd spent together since?

It suddenly seemed too impossibly cruel that they should have parted because of a complete misconception, and Alison put her hand to her head, swaying slightly. A foggy feeling filled her mind and her legs suddenly gave way, until she realised Sam was holding her and lowering her into the chair.

'Sam…' she breathed, trying to ward off the faint, 'Sam…why didn't you—?' but the tide of emotion was preventing speech and she closed her eyes, praying that she wouldn't pass out.

Much later, Alison felt she could have handled the situation better. The old saying about being wise after the event was probably very true in her case. Had not Hector walked into the office at that moment and created such a fuss, she would have forced herself to resume her duties and see her list of patients.

It was, however, by Hector's firm decree that when she had recovered sufficiently she should go home. 'We want you fit and well for the August bank holiday,' he told her firmly. 'Selfishly, I have my own interests at heart when I say this. Now, come on, I'll take you home.'

Finally, to avoid more embarrassment, she gave in, though, as Hector took her arm and led her from the room, she was aware of Sam's silence in the background.

She didn't remember much of the drive home. Hector drove like the wind, assuring her that he would deliver her car later with Sam. She insisted she must go to Clare's and collect Gemma, but Hector would have none of it, instructing her to rest for the day.

Once again, she agreed. Possibly because of the need to clear her mind and bring some sort of order to the confusion of thoughts whirling there.

And it was in the garden, resting on the steamer chair under the umbrella, that she asked herself again whether she believed Charlotte Macdonald. If she did then, other than Sam's error in not revealing the details to her at the time, the conclusion must be that Sam had not been at fault.

For some while, Alison allowed the thought to drift in her mind, until gradually the defences that she had built up since their split began to disappear. Something else flowed back into their place, an emotion that had been absent as far back as Gemma's birth.

If Charlotte had ever captured Sam's attention, it hadn't been sexually. Of that she felt certain. Why, then, had their marriage come to such an unhappy end? It was a question that Alison still found hard to answer. Perhaps because the answer would involve another kind of pain—the one of looking deeply into herself and not liking what she found there.

Sam didn't come with Hector to deliver her car that afternoon. Instead, Lucy drove it back in her lunch-hour and Hector collected her, leaving Alison feeling as though, by Sam's silence, he was saying much more than he could with words.

As the days passed, Alison waited for some contact from him, hoping he would phone or call. She longed to hear his voice, to be reassured. But as time passed, she realised that something indefinable in their relationship had changed, and not for the better.

In quieter moments she attempted to analyse the events that had led up to their separation. Gradually she came to the conclusion that she would have difficulty—if she were Sam—in understanding the depression that had gripped her after Gemma's birth, which had seemed like a quicksand into which she had fallen.

'I'm leaving, Ali,' Sam had told her during their quarrel on the morning after his night's absence. 'Until you can trust me, until you are prepared to *listen*.'

He had flung the word at her, his handsome face ravaged with tiredness and pain. And with that he had walked out of the house. Carved into her heart, the words sprang back to taunt her again.

'Until you are prepared to *listen*...'

Now, as Friday approached, she was forced to accept that he had been right. She hadn't listened. Couldn't have. Or why else was she now convinced that Charlotte had spoken the truth? Now she clung to the hope that as long as she could talk to Sam she would be able to make him understand that the depression had clouded her judgement and made her so unreasonable after Gemma's birth.

It was this conviction that drove her throughout the week, spurred her on through Tuesday at Northreach, Wednesday at Kennet and a Thursday night that seemed endless.

When at last she arrived at surgery on Friday morning, no sight could have been more welcome than Sam's car parked in its usual spot. Her heart drumming, she entered Reception and hoped for a glimpse of his tall figure. A hope that was soon dashed as Lucy brought her the morning's post and the news that both Sam and Peter were already under way with their surgeries.

It was as the morning progressed and there was no sign of him either in Reception or the office that she began to suspect he was avoiding her. And when at lunchtime she made a point of going to his room, only to find it deserted, she knew her fears were confirmed.

At five o'clock, when she had finished, she hurried to check with Lucy on Sam's list.

'He was in rather a hurry,' Lucy told her with a frown, 'and left a few minutes ago.'

Certain now that something was deeply wrong, Alison hurried along the footpath towards the car park. Relief overwhelmed her as she saw Sam's car still in its usual spot. But as she ran towards it, relief turned to bitter dismay as she saw his shuttered expression at her approach.

It seemed to Alison that he would have quite easily driven off if she hadn't waved and hurried towards him. She told herself she was mistaken and the smile he eventually forced was in some way a small compensation. Even so, the conviction inside her grew that whatever had happened in that office with Charlotte Macdonald, it had changed the course of their lives.

'Sam—I must talk to you,' she said breathlessly, aware that because of her extreme agitation her summer dress was damply clinging to her body.

'I'm short on time, Ali,' he replied abruptly, looking up at her through the open window. 'Is it about Gem?'

'No—well, yes, indirectly,' she floundered. The irony was, she realised, it was now Sam who was reluctant to close the distance between them.

He frowned, then gave what she could only take as a sigh. Then, reaching across, he pushed open the passenger door.

As Alison climbed in, she had no idea what she was going to say. To add to her unease, she saw Hector and Peter leave the surgery and walk towards the car park.

'Is there somewhere we could go?' she asked quickly, and saw that Sam, too, had noted the two figures coming towards them.

Without replying, he started the engine and a moment later they had turned out of the car park. Alison sat silently, aware of his unsmiling profile. Whatever it was that she had thought she could explain, it now seemed a jumble in her mind. But when he turned down the small lane that led to the ferry, a flicker of hope burned inside her.

This was soon extinguished, however, as he parked the car by the verge and glanced at his watch. 'I have to leave by six, Ali.'

'What I have to say will only take a few moments,' she replied quietly.

Panic overwhelmed her as she climbed out of the car, waited for him to lock it, then accompanied him down the stone steps to the river.

The grass that had been drenched with rain on their previous visit was now curled and browned with heat. Only the shade beneath the willows remained lush and green. The authorities had begun to dismantle the jetty and the decaying wooden structure had been retrieved and piled on the bank. A set of tractor tyres indicated that the work was still in progress, and beyond a sign had been erected, warning people to keep away.

There were children playing on the bank and a few strollers ambled along the pathway. One family sat with a picnic on the broad stretch of grass further down and on the bend of the river two young boys were swimming in the shallow water.

It was a peaceful, summer scene and as they walked Alison attempted to compose her

thoughts, finding strength in the tranquil sur-
roundings.

'I thought you might have telephoned this
week,' she began awkwardly, then, when there
was no reply, added, 'After Charlotte
Macdonald's visit.'

'Why should I have phoned?' he answered,
thrusting his hands into his trouser pockets as
they walked. 'I've accepted the fact that you'll
tell me when it's convenient to see Gem.'

She hadn't been referring to Gemma and she
knew that he knew that. 'Sam, it's important
we talk about this—' she began.

But stopping abruptly, he rounded on her
and in his face she could see anger.

'Talking was what I had hoped to do once.
But the more I tried, Ali, the faster you re-
treated from me.'

'I know that now, Sam,' she admitted shakily, 'but something happened after Gemma. I
felt cut off and overwhelmed by responsibility.'

'Responsibility I wanted to share,' he
pointed out sharply.

'They were such ridiculously small worries,'
Alison floundered hopelessly. 'I should have
been able to cope. I'm a doctor, for goodness'
sake. Someone who should know about post-

natal depression. But I chose to deny them, Sam. I was…ashamed…of my feelings, ashamed that I couldn't deal with them…'

'Then why the hell not share them with me, Ali? I felt like an outsider—a stranger.'

'I wanted to. But you had the surgery, pressures that demanded more of you than my… my fears.'

It was then he looked at her, his dark eyes incredulous. 'Fears?' he repeated slowly. 'What fears, Alison?'

'Oh, Sam…' She hesitated, covering her mouth with her hand and struggling for control. 'I always feared that the same would happen to me as happened to Mum. That somehow our marriage would…would end in the same way…'

'You mean you thought I would behave like your father—and disappear?' he asked incredulously.

She nodded, dragging out the words. 'I thought that was what was happening the night you stayed away. I'd been so depressed. It seemed we hadn't really talked for weeks and when I found that handkerchief—'

'That damned handkerchief!' Sam exploded as he stared at her. 'I gave it to Charlotte to use—the poor girl was in a terrible state. She'd started a fit and the woman was about to give birth—prematurely. Thank God the delivery went without complication and the midwife who should have been there finally turned up. Imagine what it was like for Charlotte,' he ground out, his dark eyes glittering. 'The poor girl was forced to cope on her own, which she would have handled, no doubt—if she had been well. But when I arrived, she was blacking out, shaking, in one hell of a mess, holding onto consciousness by the skin of her teeth.'

'But why didn't you tell me?' Alison burst out.

'I did, Ali, or at least I tried to. But you wouldn't listen, remember?'

Alison shook her head miserably. 'It was just that you left home at ten and didn't come home until eight the following morning. You'd never done that before—ever. And I thought, because we were going through a bad patch—'

'You thought I would cheer myself up with a casual affair?' he demanded grimly.

'No…it wasn't like that, Sam…I…I just didn't know what was happening to me. It all seemed such a nightmare. Perhaps if we hadn't quarrelled before…'

'Over something I can't even remember,' Sam rasped angrily. 'What an absolute waste of time!'

She looked into his reproachful eyes and knew that his anger was justified. If she had admitted to her depression then, he would have understood what she was going through and none of this would be happening now.

She needed him so much. Wanted to put her arms around him and hold him tight and never let him go. 'Sam, I'm sorry. That's what I needed to say. I had to tell you—'

'Because you now believe I'm innocent?' he asked coolly, his face tight and drawn.

'Sam, postnatal depression is no excuse, I know—'

'Ali, you once asked me if I expected forgiveness,' he cut in, his dark eyes staring down at her. 'I replied that if forgiveness was what was needed to save our marriage, then my answer was yes. Unfortunately, at the time you disagreed.'

He paused, his gaze moving over her anguished face. 'A lot's happened, Ali. I've come to accept that you don't love me...' He took a breath, adding quickly, 'Gemma will always take priority in my life. But that Charlotte Macdonald's appearance has suddenly convinced you our marriage was worth saving speaks volumes for the trust you had in me.'

It was all she could do to look at him as tears filled her eyes and she forced them back. It was clear that he had no desire to listen to anything more that she might have to say, and as he turned to go she spoke in desperation.

'Sam, are you seeing someone?' she asked shakily.

Whatever it was that he was thinking he kept to himself as a look of surprise quickly entered his eyes.

'Would it make any difference to you if I was?' he asked instead.

'I...I don't know...'

'So what does that mean?' he prompted, curiosity now filling his face.

'Just that,' she said as levelly as she could. 'Now that we've spoken as frankly as this, I think we have to consider...consider the possibility that each of us...' she stopped, clenching her hands as once again she floundered for words.

'Will find new partners?' he supplied flatly, and she looked away from his incisive stare. 'I need love in my life, Ali,' he told her, his voice shuddering with emotion. 'I'm a passionate man. Sex has always been good between us, but I need more than physical fulfilment. I need trust. And trust is a quality that was clearly lacking in our marriage or, Alison, we wouldn't be having this conversation.'

It was a biting comment and found its mark. One which she was forced to accept as he drove her back to her car. There could be no doubt that her lack of trust had driven a wedge between them. And now...

Now it was too late.

Alison shuddered as he stopped the car and waited for her to climb out. His cold indifference indicated that he had already forged another relationship—indeed, why hadn't she realised why he'd been so eager to leave this evening? The sound of his car melted into the evening and Alison took a deep breath as the taillights disappeared from the car park.

It took no great leap of imagination to guess that he had found someone to love, and any hopes she had of mending the rift between them were now shattered.

She unlocked the car and summoned the strength to drive to Clare's to collect Gemma. Thankfully her sister had customers to serve and she was able to escape. At home, Alison refused to dwell on anything that had transpired during the day until Gemma was in bed. She couldn't let Gemma sense her unhappiness.

It was much later, therefore, when Gemma was asleep and the cottage quiet, that she allowed herself to examine in detail the past few hours.

But for all the questions she raised and all the answers she gave herself, one thought remained in her mind. She loved Sam now more than ever. She'd had proof today of his love and loyalty...

Why then, in heaven's name, hadn't she believed in him when there had been no proof— just his word?

The weekend provided Alison with some thinking time. Although the pain of Sam's rejection hurt deeply, the little voice inside her told her she had to face facts.

Her biggest fault had been in hiding the magnitude of her depression after Gemma. She should have taken Sam into her confidence. But he had been working hard to help Hector build up the practice and it had seemed unfair to burden him with her own troubles which had seemed so minor in comparison.

The time also gave her some objectivity on the subject. As bruised emotionally as she felt, on Monday morning she was determined that her personal problems with Sam would not interfere with their professional relationship.

It was with mixed feelings, therefore, that she arrived at the surgery to discover that Sam was absent. 'Dr Stewart booked ten days' holiday at the last staff meeting,' Lucy explained as she passed Alison a copy of the month's rota. 'He'll be back a week on Tuesday.'

Alison felt her cheeks warm under Lucy's stare. 'Oh, yes, it slipped my mind.' She nodded vaguely. 'Well, I hope the weather stays good…'

'That's one thing about Paris.' Lucy grinned. 'There's so much to see and do there, even if it rains. It's such a romantic city…'

Alison smiled, hiding her surprise. 'Paris…yes…yes, of course.' She took the morning's post and inclined her head. 'I'll let you know when I'm ready, Lucy. Oh, by the way…' She hesitated, dragging her mind back with difficulty. 'Have you see Eila Hayward?'

Lucy shook her head. 'She went to stay with her mum—which I was very surprised at. She kept saying to me she wouldn't leave the house in case Mark came back.'

Alison nodded. 'Who saw her the day after I called?'

'Dr Stewart, I think.'

Alison nodded again. 'Find me her records, would you, Lucy, before I start?'

As Alison went to her room, she wondered why she hadn't thought to look at the rota for this week. She had forgotten that Sam had booked time off. It had come as a surprise—and a blow—that he was going to Paris. They had honeymooned there and it was a city they had always wanted to visit again. In fact, they had planned to, yet now he was going there and it certainly wouldn't be alone.

Paris was a city for lovers—as Lucy had remarked, a romantic city. Her spirits plummeted, despite her weekend pep-talk.

It proved more difficult than she thought as she read Sam's notes on Eila. His careful attention to detail and the remarks that he noted on Eila's state of mind served only to remind Alison of his commitment to medicine and his patients. The three entries on different dates, one very late in the evening when he had called to visit Eila, indicated his deep concern for her well-being.

It was evident that Sam's encouragement had helped persuade Eila to go away with her mother. And it was with interest and relief that Alison read of Mary Flynn's phone call to say that Eila and the baby were doing well in her care.

Sliding the paper records back into their envelope, Alison heaved a deep sigh. This wouldn't do. She had to focus on work. Perhaps Sam being away was a good thing after all. There would be no emotional distractions, and for that she was thankful.

The day took a turn for the better then, despite the arrival of her first patient, Victoria Reid. The fourteen-year-old was unaccompanied by her mother this time, and wasted no time in indignantly telling Alison what was wrong.

'I had a big fight with Mum last night,' she explained truculently. 'She found some condoms in my drawer and went ballistic. She said that my glandular fever started with me kissing my boyfriend and that if I was having sex it would probably make it worse. So I've come to you to find out the truth.'

'Are you in a relationship?' Alison asked, wondering what Mrs Reid had been thinking of, threatening her daughter in this way.

'Not really that serious,' replied Victoria with a shrug. 'We've only been going out for three months, just before I got the glandular fever. We haven't actually slept together,' Victoria added as her cheeks flushed, 'but a lot of my friends have sex. One of them gave me the condoms. Everyone knows it's best to have safe sex.'

'Yes, it is, but the question that's most important is whether to have sex at all in the first place. Added to which, you do have glandular fever.'

At this Victoria looked defiant. 'Was it my boyfriend that gave it to me?' she demanded.

'The answer to that, I'm afraid, we don't know.'

'So Mum is wrong, then?'

'Not entirely. Each year, tens of thousands of young people like you develop glandular fever. Kissing is thought to be a common method of transmitting the virus.'

'But I thought that was an old wives' tale.'

Alison paused. 'No, it's quite true. But not every kiss spreads the virus, though once the virus is in the body it multiplies in the cells that form part of your immune system. That's why we did a blood test. The results showed atypical lymphocytes in your blood—proof that the virus is there.'

It was clear this explanation had an effect, as the teenager sat quietly in her chair, chewing a long strand of hair that she twirled between her fingers. 'It doesn't sound very nice when you put it like that.'

'Which is why your mother is worried for you, Victoria. How did the argument begin?'

'I wanted to go to a pop concert and my mum said I hadn't rested enough. And then it just went from one thing to another.'

'Do you still feel sleepy during the day or a bit low sometimes, tearful even?'

Victoria looked down at her hands clasped in her lap. 'Well, yes. That's why I wanted to go to the concert. To cheer myself up.'

'Well, it's likely you still have the virus. I'm afraid it's only time that will see the back of it. And it's not quite two months since I first saw you. So my advice would be to wait until you feel a hundred per cent better. It will be worth it in the long run, I promise.'

Victoria nodded slowly. 'Was Mum right about the sex bit, though?'

Alison hesitated. 'I think what Mum meant was that your disease develops only if the virus is encountered for the first time in adolescence. And naturally she links the kissing with petting and petting with sex.'

'But it's not like that,' Victoria protested 'Mum doesn't understand. She's really suspicious since she got divorced.'

'Only because she now has to handle things on her own and that can be frightening for adults.'

'Well, I'm never going to get married,' Victoria stated flatly.

'Maybe not,' Alison said gently. 'But I can assure you that one day you will experience falling in love and want things to be perfect, and not have any regrets about what you may have done—ill-advisedly—in the past.'

Victoria pushed back her dark brown hair and sighed. 'Actually, I don't really fancy my boyfriend all that much. But I don't want Mum to think I've broken with him because she doesn't like him.'

'Then why don't you explain you won't be going out with your boyfriend until you feel better? Mum will probably be relieved you've talked to her and you'll recover more quickly because you'll be less stressed.'

Victoria nodded slowly. 'I could try, I suppose.'

When her young patient had left, Alison leaned her chin on her hand and stared out of the window. Heaven help her if Gemma got involved with a boy at fourteen. It hardly seemed out of childhood. Yet here was Victoria, considering sex because her friends were apparently sleeping with boys. Not because she loved her boyfriend or even remotely liked him.

How would she ever cope if she had to handle a situation like that on her own as Mrs Reid had to? For a brief moment she closed her eyes and swallowed on the ache inside her. If she needed Sam now, how much more would she need him then?

CHAPTER ELEVEN

SOMEHOW she got through the week, but on Friday a postcard arrived from Paris. It was addressed to both her and Gem. The view on the front was of the Eiffel Tower on a bright, sunny day. 'Hi from Paris' was all that was written in Sam's handwriting.

On Saturday afternoon Clare called, and Alison showed her the card.

'Did you know he was going to Paris?' Clare turned the card over in her hands.

'No,' Alison replied as they sat in the kitchen, while Gemma was napping.

'He didn't tell you?' Clare asked, sipping her drink.

'No, I'd forgotten he had time off in August, but...'

'But what?' Clare frowned.

Alison looked under her lashes. 'I discovered I was wrong about Charlotte Macdonald and...and Sam. They didn't have an affair.'

'Whatever do you mean?' Clare gasped, her eyes widening.

'Well, Charlotte came to the surgery,' Alison said quietly, and Clare's mouth dropped open as Alison slowly related the story.

'And you believe her?' Clare asked breathlessly at the end of it.

'Yes, I do.' Alison nodded. 'I just feel terrible about it all, Clare. And I don't think Sam will ever forgive me for what happened.'

Clare lowered her drink to the table. 'Ali, you were ill—terribly depressed. It was because you and Sam weren't communicating that the misunderstanding happened—not because you didn't love each other.'

'But, Clare, I can't believe that Sam still has feelings for me.'

'Why are you so convinced, Ali?'

'Because he's moved on and formed a new relationship,' she answered quietly.

'You're *certain* of this?' Clare demanded, her expression revealing her surprise.

Alison paused. 'He said on several occasions that he had to leave Gemma and be away by a given time. Then this holiday in Paris…'

'But perhaps he's visiting friends or colleagues?'

'Then why say so little on the card?'

'Maybe he didn't know what to say.'

Alison sat back and drew her forefinger around the rim of the mug. 'I think too much has happened between us. It's only reasonable to assume that in the time we've been apart he has found someone else.'

'He might think the same about you,' Clare pointed out firmly.

Alison looked up in surprise. 'I've given him no reason to think that.'

'He was in Australia for ten months, Ali. He had no way of knowing that you weren't seeing someone. And to be fair, you haven't encouraged him to call here without making arrangements first.'

Alison frowned, looking into her sister's eyes. 'Has he said something to you, Clare?'

'No, but...' It was Clare's turn to pause. 'He did mention something whilst he was helping Robbie...that he didn't like to call here unless invited...because you might have company.'

Alison shrugged. 'And so...?'

Clare sighed and rolled her eyes. 'And then he asked Robbie if you were involved again.'

'Why didn't you tell me?' Alison demanded.

'Because you would have said what business was it of his and probably got very cross.' Clare gave another heavy sigh. 'Honestly, Ali, you both should get your act together. It's not me you should be talking to but Sam.'

'I've tried,' she muttered as she stood up. 'But he's made it plain he doesn't want to know.'

'Then try again,' Clare said easily. 'All he can do is dent your pride.'

'What pride?' Alison snorted. 'I've none left to dent!'

Kerry Ames sat in the chair beside Alison's desk, with a checklist balanced on her knee. After asking Alison for two bronchodilators, she struck the items off with a pencil and looked up at Alison.

'Whew! I didn't think there were so many things to remember.'

'Will two be sufficient to take with you?' Alison asked as she entered the prescription on her computer.

'Yes. One is for my luggage and one I'll carry in my jeans pocket. Dr Stewart suggested that I should have a spare should my luggage go astray.' She laughed lightly. 'Not that I've the remotest intention of using either of them.'

'No, but it's best to be prepared,' Alison said as she handed Kerry the prescription.

'How's the breathing technique coming along?'

'Excellent.' Kerry shrugged. 'I practise a couple of times a day as a preventative now. I've not had an attack since before the course.'

'And how long do you expect to be away?'

'A year. I'm travelling with a friend and staying with my aunt in Perth.' She reached into her backpack and brought out an envelope. 'I wonder if you could give this to Dr Stewart? It's a note to thank him for all he did for me.'

Alison took the envelope and placed it on her desk. 'I'm glad you found the technique helpful.'

'Well, it's thanks to you for suggesting it, Dr Stewart...' The young woman paused. 'It seems funny, calling you Dr Stewart as well. It isn't a coincidence, is it? You are married to the other Dr Stewart, aren't you?'

Alison hesitated. 'We're separated.'

'Oh—I'm sorry,' Kerry said at once, blushing. 'I didn't realise...'

'It's an easy mistake to make,' Alison said kindly.

'It's just that the two of you seem—well, if you don't mind me saying—the perfect couple. I mean, it was you who recommended me to

Dr Stewart and he certainly worked a major miracle with my asthma and also that young boy—Thomas Knight? His asthma has really improved. I saw him in the village and he said that after the course ended, he was slowly decreasing the steroids, too. We both thought that you and Dr Stewart…were…well, a really ace team.'

It was Alison's turn to blush and she smiled. 'That's very sweet of you, Kerry.'

For an uncomfortable moment Alison thought Kerry was about to ask another question, but thankfully the young woman stood up and heaved her backpack on.

'See you in about a year, Dr Stewart,' she said with a laugh as she walked to the door.

'Take care, Kerry.'

After she had gone, Alison stared at the white envelope on her desk, deep in thought. Most patients were too polite to ask about her and Sam's relationship, although she had fielded one or two of the more direct questions since Sam had rejoined the practice. But Kerry's innocent enquiry had caused Alison to recall the times before Gemma's birth that she had been able to admit that she and Sam were not only colleagues but husband and wife as well.

It was with a deep sigh that she allowed her eyes to linger on the note. Sam was due to return tomorrow, so should she leave it on his desk this evening? Or take it with her? She could ring Sam tomorrow evening after her day at Northreach and explain what Kerry had said. It was a special letter after all. Sam had worked a major miracle in Kerry's eyes...

Sliding the envelope into her bag, Alison was about to press the buzzer for her next patient when she stopped. Sitting quietly back in her chair, she closed her eyes. What was she doing? Did she really need to speak to Sam? The answer, of course, was no. She was simply using the letter as an excuse.

Wearily opening her eyes, she leaned down and removed the letter from her bag. Propping it on top of her desk, she pressed the buzzer. How easy it was to deceive oneself, she reflected as she waited for the door to open.

And how foolish.

Alison's Tuesday at Northreach passed quickly enough as Christine Morgan's efforts to transfer her patients to the new town practice had shown results so Alison had only a small list.

She was free by four in the afternoon and home with Gemma by five. The answering machine showed no recorded calls and it was with a sense of dismay that she tucked Gemma into bed that night.

Sam hadn't seen Gemma for almost two weeks. Despite the failure of their relationship, Gemma shouldn't be allowed to suffer, Alison decided irritably. But when she herself climbed into bed, she told herself that tomorrow she wouldn't dwell on a state of affairs she could do nothing to change.

She was in surgery at Kennet until two the following day, but after another morning that brought forth no call from Sam, her irritation was changing to downright anger.

Surely he was aware that Gemma was missing him?

On Thursday, Clare telephoned. 'Sam might not be back from Paris,' Clare suggested in reply to Alison's concern.

'He was due back at the surgery on Tuesday,' Alison said at once. 'And I've heard nothing to the contrary.'

'Perhaps he's waiting until tomorrow,' Clare posed. 'When he sees you.'

That afternoon, Alison took Gemma to the swimming baths. By the time they returned home it was five o'clock and no message had been left on the answering machine.

After tea the phone rang and she hurried into the hall to answer it.

'Alison, it's Hector,' said the rather hesitant voice.

'Oh, Hector...'

'Are you busy?' he asked in a tone that caused Alison to sigh softly.

'No...I thought it might be Sam, that's all.'

'Yes, of course... I won't keep you long. It's just that I rather wondered what your feelings were about Glencourt?'

For a moment there was silence and she thought perhaps they had been disconnected. 'Hector, are you there?' she asked quickly.

'Yes...yes I am.'

Alison frowned at his distracted tone. 'I'm sorry, Hector. What do you mean—my feelings?' Had Sam expressed a desire not to go to Glencourt? she wondered anxiously.

'Well, after all that's happened...'

Stiffening, Alison felt a flare of anger. Surely Sam hadn't discussed their personal problems with Hector?

'To be honest, Hector,' she replied crisply, 'I'd quite forgotten about Glencourt until this moment.'

'That's understandable,' Hector agreed at once. 'It was just that in the circumstances

Annie would have asked you both at another time.'

'What do you mean, ''in the circumstances''?' Alison was beginning to feel that she was missing something important.

'Alison, I think we must be talking at cross-purposes,' Hector said, echoing her thoughts. 'Tell me, have you heard from Sam since Paris?'

'No,' Alison replied, puzzled that Hector should ask such a question.

'Oh, my dear—then you don't know?'

'Know what?' Alison said tightly. Her imagination went into overdrive. What was Hector about to say? Was Sam still in Paris? Had he decided to extend his holiday and not to return?

But his next words caused all Alison's concerns over Sam's silence to vanish as Hector said gently, 'Ali, my dear, Sam crashed his car just outside Heathrow. He swerved to avoid a pedestrian—and hit a blasted tree.'

For a moment, Alison couldn't speak, then very slowly she forced herself to swallow, trying to keep calm as Hector continued.

Hurriedly, Alison dressed Gemma in her dungarees and denim jacket, then went to change herself. Jeans and T-shirt, in this instance, simply wouldn't do. In selecting her clothes, she was more careful than usual, considering the possibility that Sam wasn't alone. Had he been with another woman in Paris?

Deciding on a long summer skirt and soft white top, she then pinned up her hair and brushed out her fringe. A little mascara, a touch of pale lipstick and she felt almost ready. One glance in the mirror, though, told her how nervous she was.

She glanced at herself again and felt suddenly overdressed. Would it be more appropriate to change back into her perfectly respectable jeans?

Eventually pride prevented her from doing so and quickly she gathered her bag. As she drove to Lamstone, she recalled her conversation with Hector. 'Cracked ribs and facial damage,' he had explained grimly. 'There was concussion, but you know Sam. He wouldn't stay longer than overnight.'

'You mean he discharged himself from hospital?' Alison had demanded.

'I'm afraid so. Though, when he rang me, he did say he was being fetched and driven home. Naturally I thought he was referring to you.'

'No, he wasn't,' Alison had said tightly, guessing who it had been, though.

'I feel very remiss,' Hector had gone on worriedly, 'not doing more, but I assumed you'd be there…and, well…that you would sort him out. I really think one of us should call round, Ali.'

She had been reluctant to offer, but eventually she had. Hector had offered to accompany her, but she'd refused. In view of Sam's attitude before leaving for Paris and from the remarks he had made to Hector, he was obviously not alone in the flat. Not that Hector would have been tactless enough to have remarked on that, but she felt she would be able to handle the meeting better without his presence.

What injuries had Sam sustained? she wondered. Would his companion be able to deal with them? Was she perhaps a doctor, too? Suddenly Alison felt she had arrived at the truth. It all made sense now. His insistence on returning home the evening after Gem's party and his refusal to linger at the jetty that night.

Alison glanced at Gemma in the back of the car. Curled in her safety seat, her eyes were closed and her blonde head drooped sideways. The evening sun sprinkled her curls with golden light and a deep ache of loneliness filled Alison. Sam's child...Sam's daughter. *Their* baby, created between them and loved so dearly. How would she cope with divorce and the knowledge that Gemma would, one day, be part of Sam's new family?

Alison looked back at the road. Her fingers clutched the steering-wheel so tightly her knuckles were white. She hardly recalled turning into Sam's lane.

Sam's flat was in a quiet courtyard of Lamstone village, and although she had never visited before, he had once explained where it was. She parked the car in a vacant space beside a set of wide, bleached white steps that led up to mews apartments fringed by a wrought-iron balcony.

Releasing Gemma from her car seat, she lifted her onto her hip and ascended the steps. Sam's flat was the last of the neat, white-painted doors with frosted windows.

Alison rang the bell and waited. There was no answer and, after ringing for a second time, she was about to leave when she heard a noise. Pausing, she narrowed her eyes through the frosted glass.

Her heart raced as a shadow approached. She saw a small, slim outline, obviously female, about her own height with long, dark hair. Alison stiffened automatically, her hands tightening around Gemma.

As the door began to open, she waited, holding her breath. Had she really done the right thing in coming? What if the woman resented her calling or, even worse, Sam did?

Without warning, as the figure emerged in a shaft of light, the door closed again with a crash. Alison jumped back, her grip tightening on Gemma's shoulders.

The person was shouting Sam's name. Then, to Alison's surprise, the letterbox flap popped open.

'Could you wait a moment, please?' a voice shouted through it.

Alison stared in bewilderment at the letterbox. A flurry of sounds erupted once more, then a series of muffled yelps.

Finally all was quiet, then a soft ripple of laughter accompanied the distinct outline of Sam's tall frame.

As the door opened, a ball of black and white fluff tumbled out and landed at Alison's feet.

'Whoa, there,' Sam yelled, attempting to restrain a bouncing puppy. Alison stared at the wriggling bundle of pink tummy and spindly legs that lay across her toes.

Holding the long, tangled lead, a young girl of about fourteen was attempting to unwind it from her jeans-clad legs. Alison recognised it as one of the extending leads she had seen some dog-walkers use.

'Sorry about the delay,' Sam apologised, glancing at her with one good eye. 'We seem to be in rather a tangle here.' The other eye, surrounded by a large purple bruise with a long sutured scar above it, looked swollen but not entirely closed. The rest of his face seemed fairly unscathed, though his movements were slow and stiff.

'You…you have a puppy?' Alison breathed as she felt the delicious curl of puppy tongue around her toes.

Sam chuckled. 'Yes, and rather an energetic little fellow he is, too.' He bent down stiffly to prevent the puppy from devouring Alison's sandals. 'As you can see, he's still totally un-trainable. Hopefully, though, not for ever, thanks to Tabitha. Tabby, this is my wife Alison and this is Gemma.'

The young girl smiled shyly as Sam took Gemma from Alison's arms and lowered her to the floor. 'Tabitha is looking after the puppy for me.' He grinned as Gemma patted the plump pink tummy.

'My mum breeds them,' Tabitha explained. 'We only live across the road.'

'He wants to make friends, sweetheart,' Sam told Gemma softly.

'Doggy!' Gemma exclaimed delightedly as Sam's dog, Spot, wriggled against her.

'We'd better go now,' Tabitha said after a while. 'I've got to help Mum with the rest of the puppies. See you tomorrow, Dr Stewart. Bye, Gemma.'

As Tabitha and the puppy disappeared, Sam raised his eyebrows at Alison. 'Before you ask, it's a long story, too long to explain here on the doorstep. Will you come in?'

'If you're not busy.' Alison hesitated as she glanced into the flat. She could see no one inside and since only the teenager and the puppy had come to the door, it didn't seem likely there was anyone else inside.

'No, not at all. As a matter of fact, I was about to phone Hector.' He smiled softly. 'I rather think it would be a mistake to come into the surgery tomorrow, looking like this.'

'What happened?' she asked anxiously as slowly and painfully Sam bent to lift Gemma into his arms.

'Oh, someone decided to jump out in front of me as I left the airport,' he murmured as he led the way in. 'Unfortunately, I demolished a tree and most of my car, avoiding them.'

'Are you hurt?' Alison asked as she followed.

'Nothing that won't mend,' he replied as they entered a large modern room with wide windows overlooking a small but flower-filled garden. Then he turned and smiled crookedly beneath his bruising. The same smile that always made her pulse race and her heart beat faster and which had lost none of its power to affect her as it suddenly became clear that he was entirely alone.

'You've nothing at all in the fridge, just a tin of puppy food.' Alison stared at the interior of a very empty fridge.

'There's cheese and a couple of rashers of bacon,' Sam said as he entered the kitchen. 'I let stocks run low before I went to Paris.'

'Did you enjoy your holiday?' she asked as she closed the refrigerator door, turning to face him.

He shrugged. 'It was a last-moment decision.'

'I gathered that, as you made no mention of it.'

'Didn't think to,' he mumbled, straightening his back. 'As I said, the destination wasn't planned.'

She sensed he didn't want to talk about it and as the silence deepened she said quickly, 'Well, you've no food, no milk. What are you going to do for meals?'

'I shall manage perfectly—' He suddenly stopped speaking as he bent forward slightly, a flash of pain etched across his face. 'Damn ribs,' he growled, turning away and sounding angry with himself.

'Oh, Sam, for goodness' sake,' she burst out, aware that he was in pain and attempting to hide it. 'Why didn't you ring me? You simply can't manage alone.'

He arched a rueful eyebrow as he straightened again. 'I'll be fine, Ali. The fractures will mend. It's just a question of time.' His eyes held hers gratefully for a few moments before he murmured. 'Look, hadn't you better go home?' He tilted his head towards the lounge where Gemma had fallen asleep on the couch. 'Gem should be at home, tucked up in bed.'

'I can't leave you like this,' she sighed, her patience exhausted. 'Come back to the cottage, at least for tonight.'

'Ali, I don't need any favours—' he began, but stopped when he saw her determined expression.

'I'm not offering any, Sam. Tomorrow I'll fill your wretchedly empty fridge with some decent food. Then you can come home and look after yourself.'

She had forgotten just what a stubborn individual he could be until at last he seemed to give in, drawing a hand slowly through his hair.

'You win,' he agreed. 'But just for tonight.'

A smile broke across his lips, a crooked, lazy smile that sent little shivers racing crazily across her chest as he finally nodded on a defeated sigh.

Gemma lay fast asleep in bed, her teddy clutched against her. Alison bent down and kissed her forehead, breathing in her baby scent. 'Goodnight, sweetheart. Sleep well,' she whispered, tucking the teddy closer.

The sound of water gurgling in the pipes told Alison that Sam was bathing. Closing Gemma's door, she went to the main bedroom.

It was a warm August evening, though perhaps with a slight chill in the air. The bedside lamp filled the room with a creamy glow and the door to the bathroom was open, just as it had been on the night of Gemma's birthday.

Sam's overnight bag was on the bed, but the light blue T-shirt and cotton chinos he had worn were thrown over a chair. She lifted them, intending to take them downstairs to the washing machine. After which she would prepare the bed in the spare room with clean sheets.

On impulse, she lifted the shirt and buried her face in its folds. The masculine scent recalled their love-making, how she would breathe against his skin and hold that breath to savour his smell. Suddenly she recalled how he had looked today, one eye swallowed in puffy purple folds of skin and the wound above barely hidden under a lock of dark hair that flopped across his forehead.

How would she have felt if the accident had been worse? If he had never come home? Laying the clothes back over the chair and with her heart beating fast, she turned slowly. Almost against her will, one hand reached out to open the bathroom door more fully.

The glass of the shower was misted with steam. His tall, tanned figure moved under the hissing water and she stared at him hungrily, just as she had on the night of Gemma's party. And so many nights before, when she had almost taken their love-making for granted.

How exquisite it had been to hold him. To slip her hands over his taut, hard body, invigorated from the shower. She had never known anything but fulfilment in his arms. And which she had missed so much after Gemma's birth. If only she had been able to talk about her depression. Not hidden it from him, like some guilty secret.

If only…

She stared at him now, lean and tanned, his long body turning under the flow of water.

'Ali? Are you there?'

She jumped guiltily and stepped back. 'Y-yes.'

'Could you pass me a towel?'

She realised she must have forgotten to leave one on the rail and hurried to the cupboard in the hall, taking out a soft white towel.

When she returned, the door to the shower was half-open, a long brown arm reaching out. 'Thanks,' he murmured huskily, slicking his dark hair wetly over his head as she handed him the towel.

Beads of water ran down his neck and broad, tanned shoulders. A dark and forbidding bruise lay under the whorls of springy black chest hair. Below, his strong, powerful legs glistened, his magnificent physique causing an answering throb deep in her own body as he thrust the towel around his slim waist.

She watched as though in a trance as his long black eyelashes swept against his bruised cheekbone. The water glistened over the swelling, softening the purple mask and the scar above it. Then, as if sensing her stare, he looked up, meeting her hungry blue eyes.

'Ali...' he whispered, frowning. 'Ali...what is it?'

She swallowed mutely and he stepped slowly from the shower, steam rising from his naked shoulders. Then suddenly she was in his arms, her body shuddering fiercely as he enveloped her in his embrace. Tears forced themselves from her eyes and spilled down her cheeks and he groaned softly as he smoothed them away.

'Ali, darling, don't cry...'

She was smiling and weeping at the same time. 'It's…it's just that it's a relief, knowing you're all right…'

'Silly girl,' he murmured, lifting her face in his wet hands and smoothing his palms over her cheeks.

'Sam, I—'

'Don't talk now,' he whispered, silencing her as he laid a finger over her mouth. 'Don't tell me anything I don't want to hear.' His voice was harsh as he drew her closer. 'Ali, let tonight be…just us…'

His lips covered hers with a passionate need as he pulled her against him, the chemistry between them stronger than ever. His fingers sought their path expertly, teasing her skin with sensual familiarity.

She could feel the slippery, corded muscles of his arms and shoulders as she ran her hands lightly over them, afraid to press too hard as he was still in some pain. He sensed her reticence and stared deeply into her eyes. 'Come to bed,' he whispered as he took her hand reassuringly.

Pulling her with him to the bed, the heat rose from his wet body. Slowly he discarded the towel, his glorious nakedness making her dizzy with need as she lay beside him.

Then he undressed her, sliding off her white top and unbuttoning her skirt, his eyes devouring her. When she lay in her lacy white bra and panties, he murmured tender words. 'You haven't changed, my darling. You're so beautiful.'

Her lips surrendered instantly to his kiss, her tongue eager to tangle with his. And it was then she knew how much she loved him, had always loved him, her body quivering as he pulled her close.

'I need you, Ali,' he told her urgently, lifting his eyes under their heavy lids.

She trembled, suddenly afraid.

'It's all right, my sweet,' he whispered, as though he had read her thoughts. 'Remember how it used to be...how wonderful it always was.'

Gently he unclipped her bra and slipped off her panties. His touch was so light, she barely felt his fingers. Her breasts spilled freely as he lowered his head and his lips enclosed the soft pink buds, tweaking them between teeth and tongue into throbbing mounds of desire.

Every bone in her body seemed to melt as he dragged himself against her. A tiny sob rose in her throat at the passage of his lips over her stomach. Trailing slowly down until the deli-

cious whip of his tongue flicked out to tease
her still more.

Time seemed of no consequence as his
hands stroked her with feather-light caresses
that made every nerve end in her body light
up. Then suddenly something snapped between
them. Urgency filled her as his whispered
kisses rained down on her naked, shuddering
body. Her hands moved to guide him, their
damp and slippery bodies coupled in fire.

He entered her with a single thrust, his
mouth never leaving hers. The need inside
them built until she could stand it no longer.
She closed around him like a velvet sheath and
they soared higher and faster until all around
her was a pulsing white force.

'I love you, Ali...' he gasped, as they flew
to climax together, their passion a violent force
that carried them as one to the crest of the
wave.

'Ali, are you awake?' Sam murmured softly as
they lay entwined together in the darkness.

His face was hidden in shadow as Alison
slithered towards him, linking her arms around
his neck.

'Yes, I'm awake,' she whispered, laying her
face close to his on the pillow.

'I need to ask you something,' he whispered as he took her into his arms in the wonderful afterglow of their love-making.

'I'll try to answer…'

He was silent and she felt his soft breath on her face. Threading his fingers through her hair, he asked softly, 'Are you sorry this happened?'

'How can you ask that?' she murmured, shivering under his touch.

'Because it's important that you didn't… didn't…' He was suddenly still and she could feel his heart beating against hers.

'Didn't what, Sam?'

'Didn't make love to me…out of pity.' She moved in surprise, attempting to sit up, but he pulled her back. 'You see, Ali, I was certain until last night that you had found someone else.'

'Whatever do you mean, Sam?'

'It was something Robbie said when I was helping him, about you having a visitor, a young man—unattached and good-looking by the sound of it—'

'You mean the Aga man?' Alison interrupted, half laughing. 'Oh, Sam, trust Robbie to get it all wrong. But surely you didn't take him seriously?'

'Well, no,' he replied doubtfully, 'but Hector did happen to mention he arrived at the cottage with the Glencourt invitation, but you had company.'

'But that was Clare,' Alison protested, reaching up to touch his face. 'Oh, my darling, there's no one, there never has been, ever.'

A long, shuddering sigh seemed to come from deep inside him. Once more he drew her hard into his arms, holding her there, quite still.

As they lay there, hot tears sprang to the corners of her eyes. 'I thought the same of you,' she admitted, pressing her lips into his hair. 'I thought you'd found someone else...even after hearing Charlotte Macdonald's story. And yesterday... When I thought you'd been to France with someone else I was convinced of it.' Gently she pushed herself away, laying her head back on the pillow. 'Then when I arrived at the flat and met Tabitha...'

'Oh, Ali, what fools we've been.'

'Hold me tight, Sam,' she urged, aching for him all over again. 'Hold me tight and never let go.'

Her plea was granted as he took her hand and placed it on the taut flatness of his abdomen, running her fingers down into the warmth beneath. She sighed aloud, as his response was all she could ever have desired.

On a cry that came from somewhere deep inside her, her hands captured him with infinite need, his chest hair scraping against her breasts as his mouth fixed on hers, his tongue moist and seductive as he began to make love to her all over again.

Later, when she woke, her first impression was that she was alone. Even before she was fully awake, her hand went out to tussle with empty sheets and her heart took a dive. Had she dreamt everything that had happened in the last twenty-four hours? Or had she really spent the whole night making love with her husband?

As she opened her eyes she heard Gemma's laughter, and relief washed through her body. Sam's laughter echoed, too, and the smell of coffee filled the house.

Then, in sudden remembrance that it was Friday and her day at surgery, she pushed back the clothes and jumped out of bed. Hurriedly she showered, combed through her wet hair, applied moisturiser and lipstick and pulled on her underwear.

As she was doing so, Sam came into the bedroom, bearing coffee.

He was dressed in a navy blue towelling robe and his eyebrows rose as he saw her. Without speaking, he lowered the mug of coffee to the bedside cabinet, then pulled her into his arms. 'Good morning,' he growled in husky tones.

She slid her arms around his neck, her fingers lying softly against his bruised cheek. 'Does it still hurt?'

'If I say yes, will you stay home?' His fingers slid beneath the lacy edge of her panties and he groaned softly.

'Gemma's up,' she whispered. 'Don't tease.'

'I'm deadly serious.'

'And so am I.' She laughed. 'Hector already has one member of staff absent.'

'At this moment, I'm not in the least bit bothered about Hector,' he whispered, playing with the clip of her bra. 'Can't we ring him and say something very important has cropped up?'

A suggestion that she didn't argue with as he silenced her with a long and hungry kiss which she had no intention of allowing to go unanswered, at least not for the next few minutes.

CHAPTER TWELVE

PETER JOHNSON had already arrived in the car park and waited for Alison to climb out of her car. 'Hi, Ali,' he greeted her, tossing back an untidy lock of blond hair that fell over his forehead. 'My goodness, you look fantastic.' His eyes ran admiringly over her slim figure and long legs, finally returning to narrow on her face. 'And don't tell me you've been up since dawn with Gem, because I simply won't believe it.'

Self-consciously she glanced down at the summer dress she was wearing, a light blue shift with a belted waist, and felt Peter's continuing stare. 'As a matter of fact, Peter, I overslept.'

'Well, you look...different somehow,' the young doctor murmured as they walked together along the towpath. 'But, then, women always do if they change their hair a bit,' he murmured vaguely, 'or whatever.'

'Are you on call or in surgery this morning?' she asked, changing the subject swiftly.

'Both,' Peter replied, glancing at his watch. 'Because Sam's not in today, I'm taking some of the overflow—as you will be, I should think.' As they approached the surgery door, he added quickly, 'By the way, how is Sam? Do you know? It was bad luck about that prang, wasn't it?'

'Yes,' Alison agreed, avoiding his gaze. 'But I don't think he'll be away for too long.'

'Oh, really?' Peter opened the door and she walked in. 'What makes you think that?'

Fortunately, Hector was standing in Reception and hailed them, effectively preventing Alison from answering. 'Alison, Peter,' he called cheerfully, 'good morning. Lucy's tacked on Sam's patients so, if you've no objection, we'll all make a brisk start. And, Peter, if there's an emergency, you're down for the call, OK?'

'Absolutely.' Peter nodded. 'Well, see you both later.' He hurried off and Alison was relieved that she had been saved the embarrassment of enquiries about Sam. However, Hector was staring at her and caught her shoulder as she turned to go.

'Sam rang me last night,' he said in a lowered voice, so that none of the girls on

Reception or patients could hear. 'Glad to hear he's OK, Ali. It went all right, did it?'

'Yes, pretty much,' she said, grateful that Sam had spoken to him and that she didn't have to fill in any details. 'He was lucky. It could have been much worse. But, then, I expect he told you.'

'Yes, more or less,' Hector murmured, and she thought she saw a faint twinkle in his eye. 'And what about you, Ali? Are you OK?'

She nodded quickly. 'Yes, perfectly, Hector. Why shouldn't I be?'

'Oh, of course, dear girl—you look fabulous. Which is why…' He stopped as a patient came between them. Lifting his eyes as the queue to the desk grew even longer, he shrugged. 'Well, I'd better let you go. Needless to say, you've got rather a challenging day ahead of you. I'll get Lucy to make you coffee before you start.'

Alison couldn't help thinking that, as usual, Hector knew a great deal more than he was saying. When she reached her room, she sat down and glanced at her list of patients, recalling Hector's warning of a challenging day.

She was grateful it was so, because ever since she and Gem had left the cottage this morning, she had begun to feel uneasy. Doubts had crept into her mind which she had tried to push away. Would one night of love-making really change anything between them? As passionate and fulfilling as their love-making was, sex was only a part of their relationship, not the whole.

So much had happened in the two years since Gemma's birth. The misunderstanding over Charlotte Macdonald and then Sam leaving for Australia. To add to this, she still didn't know the reason for his return.

He told you he loved you, a small voice inside her head protested, and she wanted to believe it. But what people said in the height of passion, common sense told her, wasn't always what they truly believed.

A fact that was to be echoed by Eila Hayward, as she entered and sat in the chair beside the desk. Her dark eyes still looked haunted as they lifted slowly to look at Alison.

'I wanted to thank you for helping me that day,' she said quietly. 'Lucy told me you came out specially. So...' She paused and took a breath. 'I thought it only fair to let you know that I've decided to divorce Mark.'

'I'm sorry,' Alison replied after a pause. 'That must have been a very difficult decision.'

'Now I've made it, I can face the future,' Eila told her. 'Mark came to see me at Mum's and suggested we give our marriage another try.'

'But you didn't want to?' Alison asked in surprise.

'I would have done anything once to keep him,' Eila said haltingly. 'But I asked him if he loved me and he couldn't bring himself to say he did. He loves Anthony and would try again for the baby's sake, but I realise that's not enough. I need him to love me, too.'

A shiver went through Alison. What if Sam didn't love her? What if too much had happened between them or, even worse, what if he was staying with her because of Gemma? She knew that if this was the case, like Eila, she wouldn't be able to live with someone who didn't truly love her. Even for Gemma's sake.

'I honestly thought I would take Mark back on any terms,' Eila was saying as Alison tuned back into the conversation. 'I felt so alone. So empty. And Anthony seemed such a responsibility. But I've lived a long time making compromises, coming a long way behind Mark's football and his affairs. I know now I have to find another way to live.'

Over the next few minutes Eila spoke of her attempts to preserve her eight-year-long marriage, believing that, after having a child, her husband would change his ways. As Alison listened she wondered what might have happened if her own marriage had been put to the test in such a way.

When Eila finally left, Alison had the impression that the road forward for Eila would be less painful than the one she had endured. Despite this, her sympathies were with the young woman who had been forced to make such a radical decision. What if she herself had been in Eila's position? What if Sam didn't truly love her? Was postnatal depression an excuse for the mistake she had made over Charlotte Macdonald?

Suddenly she ached to be in his arms, to know that he loved her and that last night hadn't been a mistake. She reached out for the telephone and dialled the cottage number.

The phone rang for some time before the answering machine connected. Her heart hammered painfully as she waited.

The automatic recording finished and she left a few words, asking him to call.

At the end of the day, she was still waiting.

The busy Friday should have been a successful day, one that stood out in her memory. A postcard from Thailand arrived in the post, telling her that Kerry Ames was spending a week there before travelling on to Australia. Despite the change in climate and a mild asthma attack on the plane, Kerry was continuing her breathing technique successfully.

Victoria Reid looked healthy and happy, appearing for a health check before returning to school. Victoria was looking forward to the new term, minus the distraction of the boyfriend, who, she explained, had disappeared from the scene.

Even Eila had finally arrived at a decision to put her life in order. And despite the overflow from Sam's clinic, conspiring to make a lunch-hour virtually non-existent, Alison finished her surgery before six. But none of this lightened her mood as she drove to Clare's, for what would she do if the cottage was empty when she arrived home?

Despite Clare's insistence that she should stay for tea, Alison refused, giving an excuse that she had shopping to do. Fortunately Robbie arrived home and she was able to escape.

When she arrived at the cottage, her tummy clenched as she stopped the car. Taking Gemma from her seat, she opened the gate and hurried to the door. Inserting her key into the lock, the door creaked open to an empty hall. Lowering Gemma to the floor, she watched her run through to the kitchen. Alison hardly dared breathe as she listened to the patter of her feet on the tiles.

Sam wasn't in the kitchen or the garden, and hope faded when Alison took Gemma to the bedroom. 'Daddy gone,' she murmured as she stood by the bed and gazed around.

No overnight bag, no shaver, no clothes.

Gemma was right. The house was empty.

'Why didn't you tell me about Sam's accident?' Clare demanded, her voice astonished on the other end of the line.

'I didn't know myself until last night,' Alison sighed, silently berating herself for not having explained events to her sister. She sank down onto the telephone seat, curling the cord around her fingers. 'And this evening…when I collected Gem. I wasn't certain if he'd still be here when I got home.'

'I knew something was wrong,' Clare said in her slightly offended tone. 'It was only by chance that a patient of Sam's came into the nursery tonight and told Robbie. Couldn't you have mentioned it when you picked up Gem?'

'Clare, you were busy,' Alison said, wishing she had now. 'There just didn't seem to be the right moment.'

'Well, I suppose not,' Clare mumbled. 'He's not there, I take it?'

'No, and somehow I didn't think he would be.' Alison swallowed. 'I had time to go over things in my mind today. And I expect he did, too. Clare, would you want Robbie to stay with you if he didn't really love you?'

'Of course I wouldn't,' Clare said at once. 'But Robbie loves me and I know that Sam loves you. He wouldn't have come all the way back from Australia, would he, if he didn't?'

Alison bit her lip. 'He's never said so, Clare.'

'Have you asked him?'

'No, but—'

'He's not like Dad,' Clare said emphatically, and Alison squirmed. 'When you realise that, Ali, you'll accept the fact Sam loves you. Anyway,' Clare continued as Alison remained silent, 'he might still phone.'

'I won't hold my breath,' Alison sighed.

'If you need a shoulder...' Clare said, not arguing the point. Which made Alison feel worse.

When her sister had rung off, Alison sat on the stool and listened to the birds outside the cottage. Even late in the evening, they still had the energy to sing. It was true what Clare had said, she thought as she listened. Underpinning all her doubts was the thought of their father and how he had simply disappeared from their lives. In some tangled way she had decided Sam was capable of that, too.

It wasn't quite dark as she walked into the kitchen. The sunset had been spectacular, shedding bright scarlet rays through the windows. The crimson globe had slipped down between the fruit trees, their silhouettes reminding her of the first year they'd been here. How Sam had stubbornly attempted to bring them back to life. And the miracle was that he had.

Like everything in the house, a memory was attached, something Sam had said or done in connection with it. A simple red brick had brought tears to her eyes. How was she going to come to terms with this final and irrevocable parting?

Rising to her feet, she made coffee, drank half, threw the rest away. She considered watching the late news, then abandoned the thought. World affairs held no interest for her. She didn't want to think about tomorrow or what she would do. She felt bereft and empty, so crushingly alone.

It was almost ten by the time she undressed and stepped under the warm water of the shower. As she did so, memories of Sam taunted her, his strong, tanned body, the wet drops falling from his shoulders as he held her in his embrace. His tongue teasing the swell of her breasts, arousing her to heights that set her on fire as her fingers slipped so deliciously over his taut, hard body.

Even now she was aroused by the memory so that she bent to steady herself against the wet wall, a soft sigh of need escaping her lips.

A sigh that suddenly turned into a gasp as her eyes flicked open, her wrist seeming to be locked in a firm male grasp. One that was so familiar that the instant of shock passed in a second, to be replaced by joy.

'Sam!' she gasped, her breath taken away. 'What are you doing?'

'Exactly what you were doing last night,' he muttered, as his dark eyes burned over her naked body. 'I was watching, until I couldn't stand watching any more.'

Her open mouth was suddenly covered with harsh, demanding lips as he stepped into the shower beside her and drew her against him. The mat of crisp black hair rasped against her breasts so that it was only then she realised he was naked, too.

The kiss went on and on and their embrace became more urgent. He was whispering so many wonderful things that she made no effort to demand where he had been, her needy body claiming its right to be satisfied as he made love to her there and then under the water.

He felt aglow in her arms, the smooth, taut contours of his body burning against her trembling skin as the water cascaded over them. Only the briefest glance at his chest told her that she must still be careful, a thought instantly dismissed as he read her mind and pulled her closer.

'I've missed you,' he growled as his mouth started its tormenting journey over her cheeks and downward over her breasts, playing an exquisite game with her senses.

'And I've missed you, too,' she groaned, arching towards him as he lifted her face, the tip of his tongue pushing between her lips, making love to her with a passion that seemed to know no bounds.

*   *   *

Alison turned lazily, stretching her arm across the warm limbs beside her. Contentment oozed like a warm river into her chest. She murmured softly as her sleep-filled eyes opened and met the liquid brown gaze that was staring intently at her—and appeared to have been doing so for some while.

'Hi, honey,' he greeted her huskily, leaning forward to kiss her love-bruised lips. He tasted sweet and warm and she shivered awake.

'What…what time is it?' she murmured sleepily, stretching against him.

'Haven't a clue. Two, three o'clockish. Does it matter?' He lifted his fingers and threaded them through her hair, trailing them down to her collarbone, dipping them in the little hollow.

She lay luxuriously still, her eyes lingering on his features and the dark pelt of hair on the pillow. Her gaze descended softly to the angry bruise which had been so violently purple yesterday and was now, thankfully, a mere shadow of its former self.

You came back,' she breathed. 'Sam… Oh, God…I thought you never would.'

He eased himself slowly up on his elbow, his dark eyes confused. 'Ali, say that again.'

She felt slightly ridiculous now. She could have bitten out her tongue the moment she'd said it. 'It doesn't matter,' she mumbled into the pillow.

'What do you mean, it doesn't matter?' he demanded softly. 'It must matter, for you to have said it.'

She bit her lip and looked up under lowered lids. 'It's just that...' she flustered, 'you weren't here when we got home, so I...I thought maybe you'd had second thoughts...'

Rather than looking alarmed, he laughed softly. 'Clever girl. I had!'

It was her turn to stare at him. '*What* second thoughts—exactly?'

'Perhaps it would be better to show you,' he said mysteriously. Astonishing her again, he climbed out of bed. She watched him disappear into the bathroom and return with two towelling bathrobes. He slipped one on and held out the other.

'But it's the middle of the night!' she protested as he hauled her from bed and slipped her arms into the sleeves. 'Sam...I don't understand.'

'You will when we get downstairs,' he muttered, dragging her towards him and silencing her with a kiss.

Downstairs, he flicked the light on in the hall. 'Shh,' he whispered.

'Why do we have to be quiet?' she hissed at his back, as she followed him to the kitchen.

'Because he'll be asleep.'

'*Who* will be asleep?'

He grabbed her hand and quietly opened the kitchen door. The hall light fell across the terracotta tiles and lit a pathway to the Aga. Beside it was a large round basket and in the basket, on a tartan blanket and fast asleep, was the puppy.

'Spot!' she exclaimed softly. 'I'd forgotten all about him.'

'Which is why,' Sam breathed as they stared in, 'I had to go and see Mrs Huntley today.'

'Who is Mrs Huntley?' Alison asked in a bewildered tone.

'The lady who bred him,' Sam told her cheerfully. 'Tabitha's mum. I caught a taxi, picked up a hire car, collected the dog and popped into the flat to get some clothes. Trouble is, everything took a bit longer with these damn ribs.'

'Oh, Sam, why didn't you leave a note or something? I phoned and I left a message, thinking you'd be here.'

He let the door close and pulled her into his arms. 'You mean you were worried about me?' he murmured, widening his eyes helplessly.

'Of course I was!'

He kissed her tenderly. 'That's nice.'

'It isn't nice. It's awful,' she protested, beating her palms on his shoulders. 'All sorts of things went through my mind.'

'Like what?' he demanded, holding her at arm's length.

'I...I don't even know why you bought a dog in the first place,' she replied irrationally, her voice rising. 'Or even if you've decided to go back to Australia. In fact, I don't even know why you went in the first place and...and...'

His eyes held hers and she was unable to contain the sob that came up from somewhere deep inside her. Gently he pulled her against him, hugging her tightly, and she clung to him.

'Oh, Ali,' he murmured into her hair, 'the only reason I went to Australia was because it was torture without you. I couldn't handle the thought of seeing you—but not being with you. It seemed less painful to go away.' His shoulders lifted on a deep sigh. 'But I soon realised it was a mistake. Another one to add to the long list of mistakes I seemed to be making in our marriage. In the end, as soon as I could get out of the hospital contract, I came home.'

He brushed her forehead with his lips. 'As for the puppy, he was meant to be…a sort of reconciliation present. For us all. As a family. However, it didn't work out quite that way. Still, I'd grown so fond of the little fellow that Mrs Huntley said she'd keep him for a while. And I was never quite able to bring myself to tell her that I didn't want him.'

Alison drew her fingers gently over his bruised cheek. Her face softened with regret. 'Oh, Sam, I'm sorry I hurt you.'

His dark eyes lingered on her lips and slowly he brought his head down, whispering, 'If you're truly sorry, then you'll show me how much.'

'Stop teasing—' she began as his mouth covered her in a deliciously hungry kiss.

'I'm in deadly earnest,' he growled as she gasped for breath.

GLENCOURT

ALISON drew aside the heavy brocade drapes and peeked out of the long Georgian window. The tall trees of the woods just beyond the gravel drive sparkled with early morning dew. In the distance, a very faint sun glittered on the lake that wound itself along the curve of the hill.

The breathtaking Oxfordshire countryside looked sumptuous. Though Annabelle Reid had apologised in advance for the early morning clatter of hooves in the courtyard below and had offered to change the suite that overlooked the stabling area, both Alison and Sam had refused. As soon as Annabelle had shown them into the rooms overlooking the courtyard and the high court walls, they had been swept away.

Now, at seven-thirty on a glorious, August bank holiday, the first group of horses moved as one swaying, velvet snake of deep browns and greys under the great stone arch and towards their exercise route over the downs.

Alison sighed with contentment. She turned to gaze once more on the room in which she stood, a feast of antique furniture, yet looking quite contemporary with walls swathed in candy-striped fabric. The five-roomed suite had replaced the two single apartments they were originally to occupy, a detail which had been tactfully brought to their notice by Hector on arrival.

'You did say you are quite happy to take the Huntingdon suite?' Hector murmured diplomatically as he and Annabelle greeted them in the Great Hall.

Alison felt her cheeks blush at the memory of Sam sliding his arm around her waist and saying that the Huntingdon would be perfectly fine. Referred to in the singular, their apartment had come as no surprise, as Annabelle had graciously led the way up the wide deep blue-carpeted staircase and shown them their rooms.

To say that the magnificently carved four-poster, complete with Glencourt's crest woven into its cover, had taken their breath away was an understatement. And the single room leading off it for Gemma had been fitted thoughtfully with both cot and single bed, plus any number of conveniences to make their stay comfortable.

On arrival yesterday at Glencourt, Alison had found herself gazing up at the beautiful English manor house, high-roofed and balustrade, with something akin to disbelief. The double storeyed wings of red brick and white sandstone, secreted in the valley carpeted with forests, had been surprise enough. But Glencourt's lavish interior had held them spellbound.

Last night they had snuggled into the folds of the huge bed, feeling, she suspected, much like the royal couples of three hundred years before, whose movements they were mirroring. Lying in one another's arms, with Gemma sleeping nearby, had been a wonderful end to a perfect day.

As Alison pulled her smooth blue silk robe around her, she closed her eyes and let mind and body absorb the historic atmosphere. To think she had almost dreaded this weekend a few weeks ago. The truth was, she had only accepted Annabelle's invitation for Hector's sake. Yet now nothing could have made her happier.

Suddenly a strong pair of arms snapped around her and her eyes flew open to her own image, reflected in a pair of deep pools of inky brown. Her sleep-tousled blonde hair fell in a soft wing across her cheek. Her wide, love-filled eyes stared back at her, glowingly happy.

Unbidden, her fingers went up to touch the fine chiselled lines of his face. They roved gently over the healing scar and teased the minute creases at the corners of his lips. With slow deliberation they followed the curve of his smile to the tip of his ear lobe.

And here they rested as she stared in silence at the man who was her husband.

'I never thought this could happen,' she whispered solemnly. 'That we could be so happy.'

'Or that we should ever make love in a bed where kings made love,' Sam replied ruefully, lifting his shoulders under the robe.

'Don't tease,' she warned, hiding her grin. 'Sam, this is very special.'

He arched one dark eyebrow. 'Hector did say the bed was,' he agreed with mock solemnity. 'And I know why.'

'Be serious,' she reproved, frowning. 'So, what else did you talk about with Hector?'

'Oh, just a few things.' He shrugged, hiding a smirk. 'You know, guys' stuff.'

'Like what?' Alison demanded curiously.

'Well, like us…getting together again. And he and Annabelle naming the day. And, er…Hector retiring.'

'Hector retiring?' she burst out, her eyes wide.

'Which would mean, of course, Peter and I have to find another partner.' His face was expressionless.

'Sam! Why didn't you tell me?'

'I am telling you, sweetheart. Now.'

'But how long have you known?'

He feigned ignorance. 'About you and me? Well, most of my adult life, I suppose. At least from the very first day I met you…'

She drummed her hands on his shoulders. 'You know I don't mean that,' she threatened laughingly.

He swept her into his arms and swung her gently round. Then, pulling her down on the long, red velvet sofa, he kissed her long and deeply. 'Dr Stewart,' he growled, trapping her amongst the cushions, 'will you be my partner in medicine, to love and obey for the rest of our long lives?'

The laughter bubbled up. 'To love perhaps, but never to obey…'

'You rebellious witch,' he muttered darkly. 'I suppose I'll have to settle for whatever I can get.'

'And anyway,' she reminded him at once, 'you haven't asked Peter about me joining, have you?'

'Well, sort of.' He looked at her under his heavy lids. 'Hector, Peter and I...er...kind of got together. You are, my sweet one, our unanimous choice.'

'You mean you've known a week and you haven't mentioned a thing?' she demanded angrily.

He grinned, rolling beside her, sliding his hand under her robe. 'I thought I'd save it as a surprise. Can you see the new brass plaque? Drs Stewart, Stewart and Johnson—fabulous!'

'I haven't said yes,' she said as a smile played on her lips. 'There's Northreach and Kennet to think about. And Gemma.'

'No problem.' He shrugged easily. 'Northreach is relocating. And Peter and I figure we can spare you to Kennet for one morning.'

'Well, thank you for being so selfless,' Alison spluttered, trying to ignore the exploratory passage of his fingers under her robe. 'And Gem?'

'Oh, Gem's easy,' he said, looking smug. 'We'll start a crèche—like Kennet. We'll be up and running in no time. You see? A bit of clear, masculine thinking can solve any problem—'

Alison picked up a cushion and hit him with it. He ducked and tugged her against him. 'What time,' he muttered into her hair, 'is that damn ride Annabelle has arranged for us?'

'Eleven,' she whispered, snaking her arms around his neck. 'And there's breakfast first.'

'What if we lock the door?' he suggested evilly. 'The lock on it is strong enough to keep out an army.'

'I expect it had to—once.' Alison grinned. 'Anyway, we can't. There's Gem.'

'She's fast asleep. I checked.'

Parting her silk robe, he slipped undone the bow at her breasts and released the wisp of silky chemise. His lips touched her and the sigh that had been waiting to escape from her lungs flowed up in a gasp of pleasure. 'A little to the right…and slightly lower,' she whispered, her voice husky with desire.

'Whatever pleases my lady,' she heard, very faintly, as her flesh tingled at the passage of his lips and the hot delight that curled its way through her, slowly, potently. And her lips curved into a smile as the thought came... obediently.

MEDICAL ROMANCE™

Large Print

Titles for the next six months...

October

A WOMAN WORTH WAITING FOR	Meredith Webber
A NURSE'S COURAGE	Jessica Matthews
THE GREEK SURGEON	Margaret Barker
DOCTOR IN NEED	Margaret O'Neill

November

THE DOCTORS' BABY	Marion Lennox
LIFE SUPPORT	Jennifer Taylor
RIVALS IN PRACTICE	Alison Roberts
EMERGENCY RESCUE	Abigail Gordon

December

A VERY SINGLE WOMAN	Caroline Anderson
THE STRANGER'S SECRET	Maggie Kingsley
HER PARTNER'S PASSION	Carol Wood
THE OUTBACK MATCH	Lucy Clark

MILLS & BOON®

0902 LP 2P P1 Medical

MEDICAL ROMANCE™

Large Print

January

EMERGENCY GROOM	Josie Metcalfe
THE MARRIAGE GAMBLE	Meredith Webber
HIS BROTHER'S SON	Jennifer Taylor
THE DOCTOR'S MISTRESS	Lilian Darcy

February

ACCIDENTAL SEDUCTION	Caroline Anderson
THE SPANISH DOCTOR	Margaret Barker
THE ER AFFAIR	Leah Martyn
EMERGENCY: DOCTOR IN NEED	Lucy Clark

March

A DOCTOR'S HONOUR	Jessica Matthews
A FAMILY OF THEIR OWN	Jennifer Taylor
PARAMEDIC PARTNERS	Abigail Gordon
A DOCTOR'S COURAGE	Gill Sanderson

MILLS & BOON®

0902 LP 2P P2 Medical